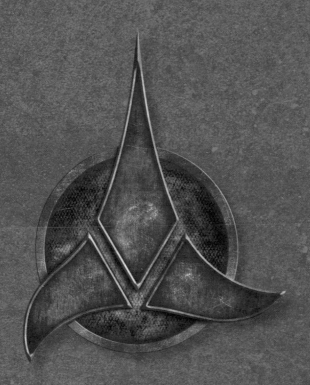

STAR TREK®

THE KLINGON™

ART OF WAR

Precepts derived from the teachings of Kahless the Unforgettable

With modern commentary by K'Ratak, son of M'Lind,

Translated into English by Keith R. A. DeCandido

Based on *Star Trek* and *Star Trek: The Next Generation*® created by Gene Roddenberry,
Star Trek: Deep Space Nine® created by Rick Berman & Michael Piller,
Star Trek: Voyager® created by Rick Berman & Michael Piller & Jeri Taylor,
and *Star Trek: Enterprise*® created by Rick Berman & Brannon Braga

Gallery Books
A Division of Simon & Schuster, Inc.
1230 Avenue of the Americas
New York, NY 10020

For information about special discounts for bulk purchases, please contact Simon & Schuster Special Sales at 1-866-506-1949 or business@simonandschuster.com.

Printed in China through Asia Pacific Offset.

10 9 8 7 6 5 4 3 2 1

Library of Congress Cataloging-in-Publication Data is available.

ISBN: 978-1-4767-5739-1

12699

Star Trek The Klingon Art of War is produced by becker&mayer! Bellevue, Washington.
www.beckermayer.com

Editor: Ben Grossblatt
Designer: Rosanna Brockley
Production coordinator: Diane Ross
Illustrator: Alan Brooks
Additional material by Dayton Ward

Special thanks to Commedia Beauregard

TABLE OF CONTENTS

TRANSLATOR'S NOTE

Throughout this translation, several Klingon titles may be mentioned that are more familiar to audiences by their English titles. However, in the interests of preserving the integrity of the work, those titles are presented herein by their original titles in the Klingon language. Footnotes will provide the English titles.

In addition, some Klingon words are left intact, either because they do not have a direct translation, or because the word rendered in English has a different connotation. Some words are rendered in the *tlhIngan Hol* style preferred by linguists, others in the Anglicized style. (For example, the "moment of clarity" mentioned in the chapter on the Fifth Precept is rendered as the Anglicized *tova'dok*, whereas the spear in a game mentioned in the same chapter is referred to by the *tlhIngan Hol* term *ghIntaq*.)

INTRODUCTION

BY K'RATAK, SON OF M'LIND

One of the great mysteries of *qeS'a'*[1] is its author. No credit was ever given on any of the copies of the text that circulated in scroll form throughout the Empire over the decades. Because of that, when the alleged "official" text was first published as a codex book in the Year of Kahless 450, it was credited directly to Kahless himself, even though no copies of the text existed until after Kahless's departure and ascension to *Sto-Vo-Kor*. Given that *qeS'a'* quotes the sacred texts, all of which were composed following Kahless's ascension, it is almost universally accepted that the long-ago publisher who collected the precepts and explications into codex form wished to increase the appeal of such a volume by attributing its authorship to Kahless. Such behavior did that publisher dishonor. (The publisher of this edition would never engage in such cowardly conduct.)

Complicating matters is the text's use as a song. In addition to being a text of precepts and explications of those precepts, *qeS'a'* is also a very popular chant. The question of which came first, the song or the text, remains an open one, and has been debated by scholars for centuries. The song itself is simply ten verses of four lines each: the precept, followed by the word *qeS'a'* repeated once. Emperor Kaldon is said to have sung the song before leading his troops into battle, and Captain Tangorq famously sang it before his battle against the Romulans at Qal-Sor.

The text itself has, of course, been published many times since 450, in many forms both physical and electronic. A course is taught on the book at the Elite Command Academy, which is required for students to graduate.

Yet still the actual author remains a mystery.

Many scholars have turned their minds to this problem, examining the text over and over again, comparing it to other contemporary writings from just after the time of Kahless.

For many turns, it was believed that Klavek, one of the authors of the *paq'batlh*[2], wrote *qeS'a'*. The *paq'batlh* was an attempt by followers of Kahless to bring together his teachings and other matters of honor into a single volume, with secondary tomes by several authors, Klavek among them. The sacred texts

---

1   The best translation for this might be "The Indispensable Advice." *qeS'a'* is often known as *The Klingon Art of War.*

2   *The Book of Honor.*

were included as part of the *paq'batlh*, but many clerics derided the second-ary tomes, including those written by Klavek, as irrelevant and presumptuous. (Klavek is the only author of a secondary tome in the *paq'batlh* who lived when *qeS'a'* was released.)

However, recent scholarship has proven that Klavek did not author *qeS'a'*. Klavek's word choices in the *paq'batlh* were radically different from what we see in *qeS'a'*. Furthermore, letters of Klavek's that were recently unearthed reveal that he had no use for this book, describing it as a "flawed volume, filled with idiocy and foolishness," based on a song he derided as "repetitive and tiresome."

Another school of thought—embodied by B'Olara, daughter of Salka, one of the leading Kahless scholars at the Imperial University—holds that it was written by the Lady Lukara after Kahless's ascension. It certainly fits in with the great work that Lukara did in ensuring that Kahless's life's work survived his departure, most notably forming the Order of the *Bat'leth*. Its members were charged with maintaining the wisdom of Kahless as the watchword of the Klingon people.

If, however, this text was by Lukara, it is the only known document written by her. What we know of Lukara comes from the sacred texts, most of which were written by Edronh, one of Kahless's followers, who became a scribe later in life, and Edronh's son Golennoq. The great lady herself wrote nothing that survived.

Except, perhaps, for *qeS'a'*. Of course, many believe that either Edronh or Golennoq was the author. There are stylistic similarities between *qeS'a'* and the sacred texts, though those similarities can be found in many writings from the time of Kahless through to the Hur'q invasion. In addition, the stories told by and of Kahless in *qeS'a'* all match those in the sacred texts, sometimes word for word.

Of course, *qeS'a'* also mentions the Hur'q invasion, so it had to have been written afterward, which means that Edronh could not have been the author, as he died during that invasion. This brings up the entire debate regarding the author-ship of the sacred texts themselves: some believe that it was only Edronh who wrote them, with Golennoq merely transcribing the words of his father; others that it was only Golennoq, but that he gave credit to his father out of respect for the stories he told him of Kahless. In his examination of *qeS'a'*, the cleric Koroth believes that the common supposition—that Edronh and Golennoq both wrote the sacred texts—is also reflected in *qeS'a'*, that in both cases, Golennoq contin-ued the work of his father after Edronh died in the Hur'q invasion.

However, the question of authorship of *qeS'a'* received another possible answer with the dissolution of the House of Gorvon. That noble House came to an end when its last member—B'Yra, the only surviving child of Gorvon—died. (Most of the House's other members were killed during the Dominion War.) Upon B'Yra's death, her lands were seized by the High Council, and in the attic of her estate, many papers were found.

One of Gorvon's ancestors, for whom he was named, was among the first inductees into the Order of the *Bat'leth*. In a chest that also contained Gorvon's *d'k tahg*, his armor, and many other possessions clearly belonging to him, were scrolls that included the entire text of *qeS'a'* written by hand. The original copies of *qeS'a'* date from during Gorvon's lifetime. Is it possible that what lay in that chest was the original manuscript?

Casting doubt on this possibility is the presence of several other scrolls, in the same hand, containing the words of epic poems from long before the time of Kahless. It is possible that Gorvon simply enjoyed transcribing works that had meaning to him. The great cleric Kas'l sang the praises of creating handwritten transcriptions of the stories of our people, believing such actions to hold great power and meaning. (Kas'l also firmly believed that Kahless himself wrote the sacred texts as well as *qeS'a'*.)

Still and all, the authorship of *qeS'a'* is of far less import than the words themselves. Whoever the author might be, that Klingon gave us a guide to living that can apply to all warriors—regardless of class or standing within the Klingon Empire. As Kahless himself said, "All life is a battle." And all those who live wage war in one way or another. *qeS'a'* provides a guide to fighting all of life's battles.

Though written centuries ago, the precepts in *qeS'a'* are still of use in today's Klingon Empire, just as the words of Kahless still ring in our hearts. Indeed, they serve as a supplement, a reinforcement of what Kahless taught us. Too often, young Klingons grow up knowing only that they should follow honor because Kahless told them to, but they don't always know what that *means*. While the sacred texts—and the *paq'batlh*—delve into honor and duty and courage and the true way of the Klingon warrior, in-depth study of them is daunting, especially for a youth.

The greatness of *qeS'a'* is that it is accessible to all. One need not be a scholar or cleric to comprehend the precepts and anecdotes contained in this tome. But it is also not simplified to platitudes a Klingon may follow by rote. Here are not bare instructions, but unfolding lessons.

Here, one can learn the true meaning of honor. Here, one can understand through the actions of Kahless, his comrades, and even his foes, as well as those who came before and after him, the role honor plays in a Klingon's life every single day.

We are warriors, but we do not fight merely to fight. We are conquerors, but we do not conquer merely to conquer. We are Klingons, and we serve the causes of honor and duty and courage, standing as an example for all the galaxy to see. The guide to how we stand—and why—can be found in this volume.

The present edition accomplishes this through stories and anecdotes, and here I have supplemented the ancient tales with newer examples. The original manuscript was written at a time when the Klingon Empire consisted only of Qo'noS, when we were just starting to explore the black sky of space, when the only alien species we had encountered were Hur'q pillagers. A millennium later, we are one of the great powers of this part of the Galaxy. We have fought and won battles against the United Federation of Planets, the Romulan Empire, the Holy Order of the Kinshaya, the Cardassian Union, the Dominion, the Borg, and the Typhon Pact.

The lessons of Kahless and the precepts that were derived from those lessons to form the body of *qeS'a'* continue to influence our lives as Klingons. The warriors of today also need guidance from stories that have actually happened in their lifetimes, or in the memories of their parents and grandparents.

And so the format of this edition is as follows: This volume is divided into ten sections, one for each of the original ten precepts of *qeS'a'*. Within those ten sections will be the precept itself, the quote from Kahless whence the precept derives, the dictum summarizing the precept, the text that accompanied the precept in the original edition, and my own commentary. As a member of a noble House, and as a prominent novelist within not only the Empire but the Galaxy at large, I have seen much, heard many stories, and encountered a wide variety of people. Those experiences have enabled me to provide the reader with familiar stories to illustrate the precepts, and also to show how these precepts play a part in Klingon life to this very day.

May the words in the rest of this tome provide all of you with the wisdom to achieve victory in the battles that life happily provides. *Qapla'*!

First Precept

Choose your enemies well.

"The wind does not respect a fool."

—Kahless

Once, the Empire was surrounded by enemies, by its own choice. It was a rock in the sea. Now it had united with two former foes against the greatest threat the Galaxy had seen to that point: the Dominion.

DICTUM: THE PROPER FOE

WARRIORS MUST REGARD THEIR ENEMIES AS HIGHLY AS THEY REGARD THEMSELVES. WITH NO ENEMY, A WARRIOR IS ONLY HALF ALIVE. THE FOE IS THE WARRIOR'S MIRROR, AND THE WARRIOR FINDS IN HIS OPPONENT THE TRUE IMAGE OF HIMSELF. WARRIORS CRAVE FOES AGAINST WHOM THEY CAN BE TESTED, THEIR LIMITS EXPOSED AND TRANSCENDED. RECOGNIZING ONE'S RIGHTFUL ENEMY IS AS SWEET AS DISCOVERING A HIDDEN PART OF ONESELF, A LONG-DORMANT DESIRE, AN AMBITION RESURGENT. FACING AND DEFEATING THIS ENEMY REFINES AND ELEVATES THE HIDDEN SELF, THE ESSENTIAL NATURE. VICTORY AGAINST AN ENEMY TOO EASILY BESTED IS FRAUDULENT, A SHAM OF HONORABLE COMBAT, AND IT REVEALS ONLY THE BLEMISH IN A WARRIOR'S HEART.

THE WALLS OF QUIN'LAT

One day, Kahless stood outside the walls of Quin'lat as a storm approached. With him was a man who refused to take shelter within that great city's walls.

Kahless went to him and asked why he remained outside the city, and the man scoffed. "I am not afraid. I will not hide my face behind stone and mortar. I will stand before the wind and make it respect me!"

While Kahless accepted the man's choice, he did not share it, and he sought the protection of Quin'lat's walls.

A day later, the storm came. Those who stayed within the city survived. The man who stood outside the city died.

No doubt the man was a great warrior with many victories to his credit before he faced the wind, but as Kahless had known, he was a fool, for he did not choose his enemy well. His vanity was polish for a poor shield.

Life is nothing if not a succession of battles, in which warriors choose their weapons, their cause, and their manner of combat.

But the most important choice they make is the enemy they fight. It is this more than anything that dictates the path a warrior will follow: wise or foolish, wreathed in victory or adorned with false glory, the subject of admiration or the object of scorn.

Only by fighting worthy foes and by engaging in combat against an enemy who tests your mettle, forcing you to strive for glory in honorable combat, do you fulfill the needs of honor.

One must not choose the enemy who will provide the easiest path to victory. Unearned victory is meaningless. Better a hard-fought defeat than a stolen triumph. A true warrior fights only those who provide a strong battle to enrich the spirit.

Hardship sweetens triumph just as comfort embitters it. A medal offered too readily is a medal unworthy of wearing.

You cannot always choose your opponent, of course. Soldiers know this, for their enemies are identified by their commanders, who point at a foe and tell their subordinates to attack.

But you can sometimes pick a battle. It is best, then, to choose wisely.

An unstoppable foe will provide only defeat, as the man at Quin'lat learned to his eternal regret. No doubt his soul still sails upon the Barge of the Dead, wishing he had chosen his life's last enemy with more skill.

THE ARENA

The invincible foe is a poor choice, but so too is the enemy against whom one can only win. While an unworthy foe will provide victory, a victory so easily won is worth little. The honor of combat is not just to achieve victory, but to enrich the spirit. If the foe be worthy, defeat brings no dishonor. As long as both combatants are strong, and do honor to their status as warriors, outcome is secondary.

Therefore, if one chooses an easy enemy against whom victory is a foregone conclusion, where then is the honor? If you win, you have not truly won anything, for the path to victory was paved with the stones of your foe's unworthiness.

Worse, if you are defeated by a foe you should have bested, what does that say about your abilities as a warrior?

Before the time of Kahless, the warlord Pohm ruled the Kir peninsula. Pohm held contests in the arena to prove he was the mightiest warrior in his realm. But Pohm always made sure the foes he faced were poor warriors. Against the lame and the sick and the old, he fought. The foes were dressed up in mighty armor and gleaming helmets. They were given the finest weapons, though they had no knowledge of how to use them.

To those who watched, Pohm seemed a mighty warrior indeed. For many turns he suffered no defeat. Every time true warriors attempted to challenge the warlord in the arena, mysterious accidents befell them, and they withdrew their challenges.

After Pohm's defeat by General Kizhar, the deception was revealed to the people. By that time, the people, perhaps sensing his dishonor, had started to turn against him.

KOPF'S CLIFF

An enemy you might one day need to rely upon is also a foolish one to make. Kahless once told the story of the two warriors who lived on Kopf's Cliff. One warrior constructed a house there with a magnificent view of the Klin Valley and the path an advancing enemy was most likely to take. He moved his family there.

The second warrior's house was lost in one of the brushfires that often ravage Kopf's Cliff. When the second warrior built a new home, he placed it in a new location, one that blocked the first warrior's sightlines of the valley.

The first warrior had other views he could enjoy, of course. But he had lost his accustomed vista and so chose to take issue with the second warrior and make an enemy of him.

Years passed, and the first warrior refused even to acknowledge his neighbor. Then one day there came the greatest fire the region had ever seen. The first warrior was not home when the fire struck, but his mate was.

The second warrior, upon seeing that his neighbor's mate would die without his assistance, went into the fire and pulled her out at the cost of his own life. The second warrior was overwhelmed by smoke and perished. The first warrior was ashamed and disgraced, for he had chosen a poor enemy, one who proved to be far greater as a friend.

The comrade with whom you quarrel today may well be the one who saves your mate tomorrow.

The Gods and the Great Tree

Enemies also change with time. Once, thousands of years before Kahless was born, Klingons worshipped gods who ruled from atop the *qo'Sor*—the Great Tree of the World, which once stood on the plains of Balduq. These gods required tribute and sacrifice, which the Klingons of the time provided, and ritual, which they followed.

Wa'Joh'a', the first god, came down from the tree to speak to the Klingons. He destroyed a village but allowed the villagers to live. He said he would rebuild the village, making it better than before, but only if the villagers killed ten *klongats* and burned them before him.

The villagers did as Wa'Joh'a' asked, though two villagers died on the hunt for the *klongat*. In return for doing as he asked, Wa'Joh'a' created a new village that was more splendid than the one he had destroyed. Brick and mortar replaced clay and dirt.

The first god even brought the two who died back to life.

Beholding Wa'Joh'a's many gifts, the Klingons of the time gladly bent their knee to him.

Seeing that the Klingons gladly provided worship, other gods came down from the *qo'Sor* to accept their due.

As time went on, the gods' demands increased. Each sacrifice the gods asked of the Klingons was harder than the last, and the gifts they gave in exchange more and more paltry.

Worse, the gods squabbled. Each god claimed a village, but some gods were jealous and demanded larger villages with more pious worshippers. The gods fought among themselves, great battles that devasted the villages over which they fought.

The Klingons became less and less interested in bending their knees to these petty, capricious creatures, or in doing their bidding.

Eventually, there came a day when Kortar the Mighty and his mate Baka visited each village and made a call to arms. After a full turn, the pair had recruited a hundred warriors for a charge across the Balduq Plains. They climbed the *qo'Sor* and slew the gods, and then they destroyed the great tree.

For Kortar and Baka and their hundred warriors had learned for themselves what Kahless would later teach: We are Klingons, and we need rely on no outside force to tell us what to do. They left the stump of the *qo'Sor* to remind us of what we no longer required and of who we are. And it was only by targeting a foe of such might that the charge on the *qo'Sor* accomplished so much.

THE HUR'Q INVASION

Sometimes the enemy that defeats you can still bring strength. When the Klingon homeworld was conquered by the Hur'q, it was a vicious, brutal defeat that almost destroyed the Klingon people. But the Hur'q left the homeworld after they plundered it. Klingons still lived.

Our people grew stronger from that defeat—their scars were their armor. For it was after the Hur'q invasion that we turned to space—another enemy we chose to battle, and one we conquered. We became a mighty empire, and it may never have happened if not for the Hur'q attack on our world. The wise warrior knows that defeat is midwife to victory.

But there is a road between the extremes of the easy foe and the insuperable one, where one picks an enemy that provides a true and proper challenge.

Through such challenges one becomes stronger and gains more honor. A worthy foe brings out the best in a warrior, regardless of the arena in which that battle is fought. The furnace of honor is stoked by glorious battle. A poor foe brings only the illusion of strength, and a warrior who fights with imagined strength cannot end any better than the man at Quin'lat. That man died without honor, the fate that waits for all who do not choose their enemies well.

K'RATAK'S COMMENTARY

This precept is one that applies across the entirety of Klingon life, from the highest seat in the council chambers to the lowliest menial worker in the slums of Krennla. It seems, at first, one that is both obvious and impossible to follow. After all, enemies are not like articles of clothing one can choose off a rack. They can appear without warning and without recourse.

The story of Kortar the Mighty and the death of the gods is telling, for it shows that even a divine enemy can be defeated if one is worthy. But I also admire the story because it reminds me of an even greater lesson that derives from this precept.

Tarrant, the great opera composer from the time of Chancellor Sturka, found himself in a peculiar situation. One of the greatest opera singers of that era was Qaov. He toiled in obscurity for many years. Then he was abruptly forced into the lead male role in *Aktuh and Melota,* when the original lead quit the opera to join the Defense Force following the death of his brother. Qaov took advantage of the opportunity, and his Aktuh was considered the definitive portrayal by many, at least until Kenni's.

When Tarrant wrote *qal yoj*,[3] Qaov assumed that, as one of the greatest opera singers, he would be given the right of first refusal for the role of Kal. But Tarrant instead gave that part to Korzol—which turned out to be his last performance, as he was killed in a duel by the mate of one of his lovers after the show closed.

(Korzol was another who chose a poor enemy, by bedding another Klingon's mate. The head of the opera company's crew was in a loveless union they maintained only because both were from mid-level Houses. The two Houses were strengthened by the mating, but no deeper bonds sustained it. However, the crew leader was very protective of this union, and when he learned that Korzol had taken his mate as a lover, he challenged Korzol and defeated him.)

Qaov was given the very strong role of Grimnar, one of the advocates, but Qaov always believed he deserved the role of Kal, and he swore never to perform in one of Tarrant's operas again.

Throughout his career, Qaov made his disdain for Tarrant well known. For his part, Tarrant had no shortage of singers who would give their fangs to perform in one of his operas, so Qaov's avoidance was of little moment.

---

3   *The Judgment of Kal.*

But Qaov also made no secret of his lifelong desire to play the role of Kortar the Mighty. In fact, midway through his career, he began a tradition every *yobta yupma*[4] of performing a dramatic reading of Kohn the Brilliant's epic poem *qo'Sor luQaw' qotar baqa je*.[5] He performed the reading all over the Empire, but his most famous recitations were the ones he gave at the stump in Balduq that is all that remains of the *qo'Sor*.

And then came the day when Tarrant announced that his next opera would be called *Qunpu' choS*,[6] and while the primary lead would be Wa'Joh'a', the first god, the second leads were Kortar and Baka. But Qaov had declared Tarrant his enemy, had declared—repeatedly—that there was no circumstance under which he would perform one of Tarrant's operas again.

Some opera scholars believe that Tarrant's choice to write *Qunpu' choS* was deliberate, done to provoke Qaov, to taunt him with two contradictory choices. Whether it was or not, he showed that Qaov was a fool to make an enemy of him, for it kept Qaov from his heart's desire. The night that *Qunpu' choS* opened at the amphitheater at Krennla, Qaov committed *Mauk-to'Vor* in his home.

It is unwise to choose an enemy who wields a weapon against which you have no defense. Qaov believed Tarrant stole his honor by not casting him in the role he desired, but in truth Qaov committed that act of thievery himself through his resentment of Tarrant's choice. And Tarrant was able to wield it as a weapon as lethal as any *bat'leth*.

The story of Kortar and Baka's triumph over the gods teaches us that what seems the wrong choice of enemy can be the right one, whereas the story of Qaov and Tarrant reminds us that what seems to be the right enemy can be very much the wrong one.

Of course, choosing an incorrect enemy can prove fatal. Perhaps this was never better illustrated than on the fateful day in the Year of Kahless 998 when the Empire invaded Cardassia, believing the leaders of the Cardassian Union had been suborned by the shape-changing Founders of the Dominion. The Empire chose two enemies that day—not just Cardassia, but also the Federation, our staunch allies of many turns' standing, who condemned our invasion, resulting in a sundering of the decades-old alliance between our two nations.

---

4   The Klingon harvest festival, an important holiday among some families and in Klingon farming enclaves, though less important than in older times, before the Empire expanded beyond Qo'noS.

5   *Kortar and Baka and the Destruction of the Great Tree.*

6   *Twilight of the Gods.*

Chancellor Gowron chose poorly in doubling his enemies. Of course, we now know that a Founder whispered in his ear the entire time: a Changeling had replaced General Martok, advising him to go forward with the foolish invasion—an invasion that was not even successful! The Empire did not conquer Cardassia, and we remained in conflict with them and with the Federation for several turns.

Not that Chancellor Gowron was wrong; he was simply premature, for eventually Cardassia *was* taken over by the Dominion. By that time, the Martok Changeling had been exposed on Ty'Gokor by Gowron, and the real Martok was returned to the Klingons after he escaped from a Dominion prison. Only then did Chancellor Gowron realize his error in making the Federation his enemy. At that point, the chancellor realized his mistake and finally heeded the words of Kahless. The wind—the massing force against which there is no defense—was once more an ally. The Khitomer Accords were restored, and Klingons and the Federation became stalwart allies once more. Together, the two nations faced the Dominion in many a mighty battle.

So many statues in the Hall of Warriors were erected for those who fought bravely against the Dominion: Kor, the *Dahar* Master, who kept ten Jem'Hadar vessels at bay with but a single Bird-of-Prey; K'Temoc, who held the line at Bolarus; Woktar, whose daring maneuvers after his captain was killed led to victory at Hanovra; B'Entra, who discovered how to counter the Breen energy-dampening weapon; Klag, who singlehandedly fought off a dozen Jem'Hadar at Marcan V; Mavlaq, who led the raid on the ketracel-white facility on Pelosa Minor; Kartok, who led the forces that took Raknal V; H'vis, who discovered the sabotage of Captain Goluk's fleet; and, of course, Martok himself, who ascended to the chancellor's chair by the war's end and has led us ever since. Let their names echo evermore!

Tellingly, no statues were erected in the Hall for heroism against the Cardassians or the Federation from 998–999.

Eventually, even the Romulans joined the war effort. In the past, both the Federation and the Romulans were our enemies. Who can forget the vicious battles fought against the former at Donatu V or against the latter at Klach D'Kel Bracht? But the Empire accepted the Federation's help after the Praxis disaster, which led to the Khitomer Accords. The Romulans had been our allies in the past, though it was often an alliance of convenience against a common enemy. At one time that enemy was the Federation, and more recently, it was the Dominion.

Once, the Empire was surrounded by enemies, by its own choice. It was a rock in the sea. Now it had united with two former foes against the greatest threat the Galaxy had seen to that point: the Dominion. United, the three nations were able to turn the tide of the war and bring the Dominion to ignominious defeat in one of the greatest victories in our empire's grand history.

The day when Chancellor Martok stood alongside Federation and Romulan soldiers on the desolate ruins of Cardassia Prime was one of the greatest the Empire had ever seen. And it came about because the leaders of the Empire chose the right enemy, and the right time to sift amity from the dregs of enmity.

Another example of this precept's value comes from my own career. My first novel was *qul naj*,[7] and upon its release, it was generally praised. The book remains readily available to this day and is one of the most read books in the Empire. Some were, naturally, less than fond of it, for such is the nature of art that it is not seen the same way by all. However, those critics who disparaged my work were critical only of the work itself, not of me as a Klingon. It was only the text they found disagreeable, and they said so in their commentaries.

There was, however, one exception. I will not honor this particular *petaQ*[8] by naming him, but suffice it to say that he was not satisfied with simply enumerating the flaws he perceived in *qul naj*. No, he also besmirched my honor, belittled my parentage, and questioned my motives. When *yoj nIyma'*[9] was published two turns later, this critic took things a step further and spoke poorly of my mate at the time.

That critic chose me as an enemy. I would not have chosen him—the artist who chooses a critic as an enemy is a fool, for such foes are unworthy under the best of circumstances. Indeed, there is a valuable lesson in that. It is obvious that choosing an enemy whom one cannot defeat is unwise, but not so obvious is that choosing a foe whose defeat brings you nothing is equally pointless. While I would have been completely within my rights to seek him out and challenge him to a duel, I did not see any reason to waste my time to do so. (I had never directly encountered him in person.) Indeed, the duel would have accomplished nothing. My book was a success, and this particular commentary did little to affect my reputation. Indeed, the critic's comments said more about him than

---

7 *The Dream of the Fire.*

8 This strong insult has no direct translation.

9 *The Vision of Judgment.*

they did about me. So if I defeated him, it would have done no more to enhance my honor than stepping on a *glob* fly. And if he defeated me, the Empire would lose any art I might create in the future, while my victory would cost the Empire only a critic. Between us, we exemplified both sides of this precept: aim neither too high nor too low.

I would have thought nothing of this *toDSaH*,[10] but for my later encounter with him at the celebration hosted by my publisher upon the release of *poH bIrqu' SuvwI'pu'*.[11] He approached me and said he had just finished a novel of his own, and he had the temerity to ask me for advice and possibly for editorial input.

At that point, I had little choice but to kill the fool. He was baffled by my challenge and was utterly unprepared for it. Barely was he able even to defend himself, as he had absolutely no comprehension of the fact that he had made an enemy of me many turns earlier. I did not choose him as an enemy, but he chose me, and he did not live to regret that choice.

Councillor K'Tal, who served on the High Council from the days of Chancellor Ditagh until shortly after the Dominion War, told a story once at a feast in his honor. When he was growing up in the First City, he would always purchase *jInjoq* bread from a small bakery. Every morning, K'Tal would enter the shop at the same time as a cantankerous old Klingon. Barely able to walk, this old warrior would enter the shop and berate the proprietor for several minutes, casting aspersions on his parentage, his mate, his choice in clothing, the state of his shop, and anything else that came to mind.

But then, after a lengthy harangue—the same diatribe as on every other day, but robed in different words—the old man would purchase seven loaves of *jInjoq* and be on his way.

At first, K'Tal was incensed. He asked the baker, "Why do you allow him to insult you so? His words boil my blood, and they were not even directed at me!" But the baker chuckled and said, "He is my best customer. Every day he buys seven loaves of *jInjoq*, except on holidays, when he buys ten. I could choose to accept his insults and challenge him. Given his age and infirmity, victory would easily be mine. But then seven loaves of *jInjoq* would rot on the shelves every day, and I would be denied the entertainment of hearing what new insults he had for me."

---

10   An insult roughly equivalent to *idiot.*

11   *Warriors of the Deep Winter.*

K'Tal said he learned a lesson about the treacherous waters of politics that day. The old man tried to goad the baker into becoming his enemy, but the baker chose more sensibly than that. Making an enemy of the old man would not have furthered the cause of honor, would not have improved his standing within the community, would not have accomplished much of anything except to end a morning ritual that the baker had actually come to appreciate.

Honor is served only by combat that elevates the spirit. Correct choices—of whom we fight, and why, and how we live—are paving stones. Taken together, they can make a road we travel to reach honor. Choosing unworthy foes such as the critic or the old man creates a road to futility; choosing foes such as Tarrant or the Federation can erect not a road, but a wall that keeps one from entering the domain of honor. Only worthy foes like the Dominion or the gods themselves bring a warrior glory and honor.

SECOND PRECEPT

STRIKE QUICKLY OR STRIKE NOT.

"Four thousand throats may be cut in a single night by a running man."

—KAHLESS

Carrying just his *d'k tahg,* Krim climbed the mountain with the stealth available only to a single unencumbered warrior. He ran across the battlements, slashing the throat of each sentry.

DICTUM: THE BOLD STRIKE

WARRIORS MUST EXALT UNFETTERED ACTION. WHILE COUNCILLORS DISCUSS AND SCHOLARS DEBATE, WARRIORS ACT. THE HARMONIOUS WARRIOR—THE WARRIOR ALWAYS MARCHING TOWARD THAT WHICH CONFERS HONOR—DOES NOT HESITATE. ACTION TAKEN WITHOUT UNDUE CONSIDERATION IS PURE, AND WARRIORS SEEK PURITY. PURITY OF ACTION, PURITY OF PURPOSE. WHEN THE FEAR OF DANGER LOOMS, WISE WARRIORS WILL ASSAIL IT. WHEN THE THOUGHT OF FAILURE CREEPS, NOBLE WARRIORS WILL BANISH IT. THUS PURGED OF DOUBT, A WARRIOR'S MIND IS LIGHT AS SMOKE. QUIET MINDS FREE OF DELIBERATION CONSTRUCT NO OBSTACLES BETWEEN WARRIORS AND THEIR AIMS. CLEAR MINDS DO NOT IMPEDE THE WILL, THE PRIMARY INSTRUMENT OF A WARRIOR'S POWER.

THE WARLORD OF THE MOUNTAIN

A fast strike to the heart will provide victory far quicker and more easily than a protracted battle. All the technique in the world will not aid a warrior fallen in combat.

If the battle is just, the cause glorious, and the enemy worthy, then honor comes from victory. While there can be honor in defeat, there is more in victory. At its simplest, battle is done in order to win.

A warrior surveys the field of battle and finds the way to victory. Often, the best way to a destination is the shortest.

Kahless's goal was to unite our people. His was a path paved with pain. There were no short paths to that victory, as many warlords would not bend their knees to Kahless. They resisted his message of glory, they cast aside his call to honor, and they scoffed at his promise of unity.

One of the most recalcitrant of these was Ralkror, the Warlord of Kol'vat, who ruled from Goqlath Mountain.

For centuries, Kol'vat stood undefeated, for any who tried to lay siege to it would first have to climb the mountain. Even the most foolish of rulers knew to put sentries around the periphery of the mountaintop, thus providing the rulers of Kol'vat plenty of warning to mount a defense.

Ralkror had ruled for many turns and had never been defeated. Indeed, he was never in any danger of being defeated. Four thousand warriors stood on the battlements of Goqlath, ready to defend Kol'vat against any foolish enough to attempt conquest.

Repeated victory brings arrogance. And idle hands forget how to grip the hilt. Ralkror saw no reason to heed the words of Kahless, nor allow himself to accept the wisdom of those words. He was Ralkror the Mighty. What need had he to capitulate? He had four thousand troops posted on the battlements who would see any attack coming.

The *wam* serpent can safely ignore the plotting of *gagh*. That is how Ralkror saw his position and circumstance.

Warriors who believed in Kahless mounted an attack on Goqlath Mountain. They knew the history of Kol'vat, knew that no one had ever taken the mountain by direct force. But Kahless's goal, and theirs, was to unite all Klingons, even those atop Goqlath.

Led by General Tygrak, they struck from the east at dawn, when the rising sun would blind Ralkror's sentries. With the light at their backs, they attacked.

But though Tygrak's strategy was sound, he still lost the day. Even with the sun beaming behind them, Tygrak and his soldiers were defeated. Tygrak's forces retreated to the caves on the outskirts of Kol'vat.

A youth named Krim saw the flaw in Tygrak's strategy. Many had tried to storm the battlements of Goqlath Mountain. All had failed.

Words had also failed, for Kahless had sent many emissaries to Kol'vat to try to convince Ralkror of the nobility of his cause. Ralkror returned the heads of each of those emissaries to Kahless.

Fierce battle upon a mountain's face is a lengthy proposition. Krim decided on a quieter approach.

On a moonless night, while the rest of Tygrak's soldiers slept, Krim stripped off his armor. Carrying just his *d'k tahg*, he climbed the mountain with the stealth available only to a single unencumbered warrior. He ran across the battlements, slashing the throats of each of the sentries that guarded Kol'vat.

By the time one warrior saw his attacker, Krim had run past him and the warrior next to him and killed them both.

With the sentries dispatched, General Tygrak was able to do what no one had done before. He conquered Goqlath Castle, slaying Ralkror himself. To Krim, he gave the honor of presenting the warlord's severed head to Kahless. Upon making this delivery, Krim said, "This is the last head you will receive from Kol'vat."

Krim then told the story of how four thousand throats may be cut in a single night by a running man.

Instead of waiting for proper conditions to coalesce, Krim created his own conditions in his own time.

THE KORVIT TRAPS

Kahless told Krim a story of his own. His cousin was a farmer, and he lay out *korvit* traps, even though no *korvit* had been sighted for many turns. The neighboring farmer mocked Kahless's cousin. He had wasted time setting traps for an animal that would never come, the man said. He could have spent the time tilling the fields so he could better grow food. After all, that is the duty of a farmer, to provide food so warriors may fight with full bellies.

But *korvit* can be stealthy beasts, and one night, without warning, they came. Kahless's cousin's crops, surrounded by the bodies of dead *korvit*, were untouched. The neighbor's fields were ravaged, for the *korvit* gorged on his lands.

The neighbor did eventually place traps, but his yield was a quarter of the cousin's harvest. Starting a battle after the enemy has already won is a waste.

Krim thought he understood Kahless's story, that he himself was like Kahless's cousin. But Kahless laughed then and told Krim that Kahless's cousin was Ralkror. Or, more to the point, who Ralkror was. He anticipated the battle by posting four thousand guards. But over time, he became the neighbor. He became complacent in believing that his strategy would work forevermore.

Krim, Kahless explained, was the *korvit*.

To the first goes the triumph. Victory postponed can curdle into defeat. It is as they say: The *targ* that charges is the *targ* that eats. Opportunity is like the wind—now appearing, now vanishing. You must take before it is gone!

In the Valley of Hamar

One of the greatest battles in the history of our people was General Kizhar's campaign against the warlord Pohm. The warlord had a strong position in the Valley of Hamar, and the general had only five hundred warriors at his back. But Kizhar rode all through the day and arrived within striking distance of the valley in the middle of the night.

Pohm knew that Kizhar's troops were en route, and told his warrior to be prepared for an attack at dawn.

But Kizhar knew the way to a quick victory is to strike your opponent in the heart instantly. Who looks too long will never leap!

Though his warriors had ridden hard, he did not wait until first light to attack as expected.

Leaving their exhausted mounts behind, Kizhar's five hundred attacked swiftly on foot in the depths of the night. Kizhar refused to wait until the sun rose before engaging in a long siege he would likely lose. Instead, he caught Pohm's troops unawares, at the time *he* had chosen.

Victory comes easily to the warrior who pounces. There is no honor in attacking in secret. True warriors do not hide their faces from their foes, but surprise can be a warrior's soundest armor.

It takes courage to attempt what has not been done before. It takes cleverness and guile and audacity to go against a foe who outmatches you. On the face of it, five hundred should not defeat two thousand, nor should one defeat four thousand. But a true warrior does not accept life on its face, but shapes circumstances into new forms.

While a quick strike can yield swift triumph, the other half of the precept is also of value: There are times when a warrior should not strike at all.

THE SICKLY BROTHER AND THE STRONG

There were once two brothers who grew up in the Ketha Lowlands. The older brother was small and sickly, and the younger brother was huge and strong. It was always assumed that the younger brother would become a warrior while the older brother would remain home as the head of their meager house.

But the younger brother was constantly getting into trouble. He stole from his neighbors and he brutalized the younger children who were too small to defend themselves, and when he applied to join the Forces of Kahless, he was rejected as unworthy.

The older brother, however, worked hard to overcome his physical deficiencies. He trained in the *mok'bara* and became a warrior in the Forces of Kahless, albeit as a clerk. (Even the strongest army must have support. Every boot needs a sole.)

This infuriated the younger brother. He had assumed he would be the warrior in their family.

When the older brother came home on leave, the younger brother challenged him. This left the older brother with a dilemma: accept the challenge to a fight he could not possibly win or walk away.

He chose the latter. After all, he was the older brother. His primacy in the household was assured by his birth, reinforced by his status as a warrior, which his sibling did not possess. Even with his *mok'bara* training, his sibling was twice his size. This fight was one he could not possibly win. But it was one he *did not need* to win or even, indeed, to fight.

So he walked away. Fighting a battle you cannot win, when you have already triumphed, is like trading your *ghIntaq* spear for a rake.

An honorable challenge should never be turned down. But the younger brother's challenge was baseless. His desire to do battle with his brother had nothing to do with honor and everything to do with shame. On the field of honor, he had already lost.

The older brother recognized this. By refusing a dishonorable challenge, he preserved not only his own honor, but his brother's as well. Though angry, the younger brother was spared the stigma of defeating a foe who is incapable of fighting back.

Most important, however, is that when a warrior does choose to fight, the choice is made swiftly and without hesitation.

A tentative warrior is no warrior. When a warrior faces a challenge, there is no time to dither or think, to worry over contingencies, to wonder about outcomes. Doubt weakens iron. Action must be taken or the battle will be lost before it begins.

So take action! Let your war cry be your shield!

K'RATAK'S COMMENTARY

The saying of Kahless's that goes with this precept is one of the greatest wisdoms of our people. It is among the most oft-quoted of Kahless's many great sayings, and it comes from Krim and his attack on the four thousand who guarded Goqlath Mountain.

The most famous application of Kahless's words and Krim's actions was that of the great Captain Kraviq of the *I.K.S. Roney* a century ago. He was sent to secure the colony of Qolis, a world occupied by *jeghpu'wI'*[12] known as the Fortrans. But the Fortrans' homeworld had come under the protection of the Federation. Emboldened, the Fortrans decided it was time to take their colony back from us. Kraviq was sent to secure Qolis and to ensure that the Fortrans on that world remained under the Klingon flag.

But the Fortrans were encouraged by their new status with the Federation, and so they attacked the *Roney*, crippling it and encasing it in a tractor beam. (The Federation *claimed* to have no knowledge of how the Fortrans came into possession of Starfleet phasers and tractor beams. It was a different time, when the Federation was our blood enemy rather than the staunch allies they have been since the destruction of the moon Praxis.) Kraviq and his crew were captured and denied the honor of dying.

Knowing that reinforcements were due in two days, Kraviq bided his time. He waited for the Fortrans to take him away for interrogation—he knew that a warship captain would be so targeted—at which point he was able to over-power his captors and escape to the mountains of Qolis. But he was still alone against four thousand Fortrans. He could wait until the reinforcements arrived—but more of his warriors may have suffered ignoble deaths at the Fortrans' hands while he failed to take action. He was but one against many.

---

12   Literally, "conquered people." *jeghpu'wI'* are considered less than citizens, but more than slaves. This designation is given to the inhabitants of worlds Klingons have conquered and added to their Empire.

And then Kraviq remembered the stories he was told in his youth, of the Campaign at Kol'vat. He recalled the story of Krim, who also faced four thousand foes alone and was victorious. The honored dead raising their flags all around him, Kraviq sprang to action. Using the native flora, Kraviq was able to fashion a spear—the Fortrans had taken his *d'k tahg*—and he slit the throats of all the Fortrans. Like Krim, as soon as he came upon a strategy, he did not hesitate, but made a risky, yet glorious decision. He knew the danger, yet also knew that there was more danger in not acting.

By the time reinforcements did arrive, Kraviq had done all the work, slitting approximately four thousand throats in a single night. Kraviq himself was killed, but he was victorious. Soon thereafter, a statue of Kraviq was enshrined in the Hall of Warriors, where it still serves as a reminder of the honor won by those who act as the lightning strikes: quickly and without considering danger or the possibility of failure. Like Krim before him, Kraviq found an opportunity, seized it, and struck swiftly. Qolis remains a Klingon colony even now, a testament to Kraviq's honorable deed.

Less well known is the world of Qadyaq, which contained a uridium mine run by the House of Taklat. That House was ruined by the destruction of Praxis, and the people of Qadyaq were left destitute. The citizens of that world turned to dishonorable means to keep their planet solvent. They stole from other Klingon worlds, sacrificing their honor to save their lives—always a poor bargain. This proved a less-than-efficacious strategy, for there was one among them who was revolted by the people's thievery. Mazka was a minor government official, but he knew that a life without honor is like poison to the spirit, and a Klingon who steals from other Klingons has forfeited his right to live. So he took his *d'k tahg* and slew the people of Qadyaq by slitting all their throats in a single night.

Today, Qadyaq is an uninhabited world, a minor planet of little interest now that its uridium is depleted. Mazka's swift strike redeemed the people's honor, but it was not enough to save his world. His victory, though swift, was hollow.

Still, one need not actually slay four thousand people to demonstrate the use of deliberate action in the service of honorable victory. One of the finest tapestry makers in Klingon history is the great Danqo. His *targ*-hair tapestries decorate the walls of many of the finest Houses in the Empire, and legend has it that he hunted and killed the *targ*s himself. As his fame rose, he took on apprentices to assist him in keeping up with demand.

Apprentices to greatness often achieve their own fame. While J'Dor is not as well regarded as Danqo—no one in history is—after several turns as Danqo's primary assistant, he left the service of the great one to strike out on his own. The tapestry that adorns the entryway to the Lukara Edifice in the First City is one of J'Dor's.

In any event, J'Dor's departure led to a vacancy that needed to be filled by one of the two apprentices, Kavo and Lyja. Kavo had been with Danqo for three turns, and he assumed the position was as good as granted, seeing as Lyja had been with Danqo for only two.

Lyja, though, believed herself to be the better artisan, but she had no way to prove that to Danqo. Apprentices have no body of work of their own to show for their efforts, for they work only in service of the master. Lyja would show her master her true worth. Gathering up the spare *targ* hair, she stayed up all night working on a small tapestry displaying a warrior holding a *bat'leth* aloft. Normally, such a tapestry—even one as small as what she created—would take several days. She completed it in one night of tireless work.

The next morning, she gave the tapestry to Danqo as a gift. Kavo immediately chided her for making use of *targ* hair that was not hers to use, but Danqo was impressed with her initiative. To Lyja's delight, and Kavo's annoyance, she was given the position of primary assistant, for she acted with dispatch in formulating and executing a plan to victory. She struck swiftly, accomplishing in one night what would usually take days.

Kavo did not strike at all, and was left in defeat, to wallow in regret. That tapestry of a warrior holding a *bat'leth* aloft, small though it is, still holds a place of honor on the walls of Danqo's workshop.

More fundamentally, when in honorable combat, the best route to victory is a quick blow to one's opponent. In the darkest days of the Dominion War, Chancellor Gowron was challenged by Worf on behalf of Martok, the general who was both Gowron's chief of staff and the head of Worf's House. Gowron had ordered Martok into many unwise campaigns, knowing that they would result in failure. Though it was a time of war, the chancellor feared the general's growing popularity and took advantage of the opportunity to force him into several defeats.

Though Gowron was their commander in a time of war, Worf knew the chancellor was behaving with dishonor and leading Klingon warriors into defeat when victory was all that would keep the Dominion from spreading their pernicious influence beyond Cardassia. So Worf took the only action he could when Gowron refused to cease his schemes: he challenged the chancellor. Their battle was ferocious, worthy of song, as two of the greatest warriors of recent memory fought fiercely.

Worf was able to win even after Gowron had shattered his *bat'leth* and gained the upper hand by so doing. As the chancellor was poised to strike the final blow, Worf grabbed two shards of his broken blade and thrust them quickly into Gowron's gullet. Once more, decisive action, a chance taken in the purifying glare of unthinking haste, had changed the course of Klingon history. Worf's victory paved the way to Martok's ascension to the chancellorship, and he continues to rule us with honor.

A speedy strike blazes the path to victory, even if defeat seems imminent. Never underestimate the power of a decision made lightly, without the burden of debate, argument, or endless reasoning. Who *acts,* wins—who ponders, loses. And who wins well, wins honor.

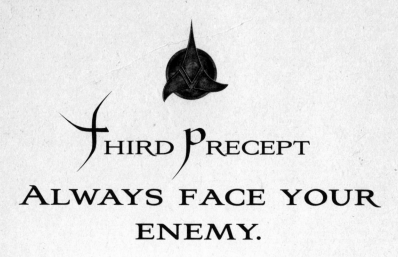

THIRD PRECEPT

ALWAYS FACE YOUR ENEMY.

"A Klingon who kills without showing his face is no Klingon at all."

—KAHLESS

Biroq's many martial triumphs included his single-handed defeat of the guards who defended the Samnatti oligarchs on Ty'Gokor, the first world outside our home system to be brought under the flag of the Klingon Empire.

DICTUM: THE TRUMPETED ARRIVAL

WARRIORS MUST ANNOUNCE THEMSELVES. PROCLAIMING THEIR INTENTIONS AND DESIRES—ENTERING TO THE TRUMPETS OF THEIR CERTAINTY—WARRIORS MAKE THEMSELVES KNOWN AT ALL TIMES.

THEIRS IS THE WAY OF HONESTY AND BACKBONE. FOR THIS REASON, THEY FORSWEAR THE SHADOWS. A WARRIOR DOES NOT WHISPER, NOR PLOT, NOR CONNIVE IN UNWITNESSED SECRECY. WARRIORS SHOW THEIR FACES AND HURRY TO CONFRONT DANGER, FEAR, AND PAIN. YOU MUST NOT HIDE.

MAKE YOUR CAUSE KNOWN TO ALL, EVEN TO YOUR ENEMY. IT IS ONLY THROUGH CANDOR, AS SIMPLE AS A BLADE, THAT YOU CAN ACHIEVE TRUE STRENGTH AND LASTING HONOR.

Of Klingons and Beasts

Honor comes through combat. True combat requires two foes, face-to-face. There is no enrichment of the spirit if you do not look your opponents in the face, if you do not see the fire in their eyes, if you do not show the fire in yours.

There is a clarity that comes from two warriors fighting each other. In combat, all artifice, all posturing, is stripped away. During the time of battle, it matters not what family one was born to. Your past deeds, or misdeeds, are of no consequence. All aspects of life are burned away in the crucible of combat, leaving only two warriors, two weapons, and the will to win. It is simply the truth of two warriors battling each other.

In those moments when warrior confronts warrior, all that is left is skill and cunning and speed and guile. Combat kindles the fire of honor that burns in a warrior's soul.

Authentic battle comes only when warriors face each other. The definition of each combatant can be found in the other's eyes.

Turning your back on a warrior is the greatest of insults. Such an action states that you do not fear your opponent, do not think your foe worthy of your attention or of combat. You display your unwillingness to show that person your face, to regard your opponent as a rightful combatant. It shows contempt for combat itself, for the very institution of war, the mother of all Klingons.

It is also foolish. Showing an enemy your back invites a backstabbing. True, this result would prove your foe cowardly, but you would be just as dead. (Blows to the back call to mind the old saying about misfortune in battle: The unlikeliest sword can still be blessed with a well-timed strike. And remember the adage: The greatest demon is luck.) Worse, you will have died disgracefully, without even seeing your opponent's face, in combat that was no combat but only the clashing of beasts.

The *klongat* will often attack its prey unawares, not giving the creature the opportunity to defend itself. The *wam* serpent slinks along the ground, hidden by the tall grass, until it rises and strikes. But we are Klingons, and our combat serves a loftier purpose, that of honor. Klingons who fight without showing their faces are no different from the lurking *klongat* and the creeping *wam* serpent. This is why *HaDI'baH*[13] is one of the greatest insults a Klingon can utter.

---

13   Animal.

THE FEARFUL WARLORD

Kahless's mate, the Lady Lukara, had a brother named Ki'Var. He served as a warrior in the army of the warlord Kranx. Under the direction of Kranx, Ki'Var won many campaigns, conquering Kopf's Cliff and Ketha for the warlord.

However, Ki'Var's victories led to his becoming very popular with the troops and the people. Kranx feared Ki'Var would rally the support of his subjects in a coup.

One night, Ki'Var came to give a report to Kranx on the conquering of Ketha. After doing so, he turned to leave. Kranx then walked up behind the warrior and thrust his blade into Ki'Var's back.

Kranx tried to declare Ki'Var a traitor, accusing him of consorting with the royal family of Ketha, who had fled into exile after Ki'Var's victory. But Ki'Var's sister, the great Lady herself, pled her brother's case. In the end, the people believed Lukara and not Kranx. Lukara led the very uprising Kranx had hoped to avoid. The warlord died in disgrace. A fool summons disaster by fearing it.

Had Kranx simply declared Ki'Var unworthy, or challenged him in honorable combat, he might have continued to rule for many turns. Indeed, Kranx was Ki'Var's commander in battle. If he ordered Ki'Var to commit *Mauk-to'Vor*, Ki'Var would have done so without hesitation.

But by refusing to show his face, by not looking his foe in the eye—by acting in darkness and forswearing the light of righteous action—Kranx sealed his fate. Where the assassin relies on subterfuge and dishonest stealth, the warrior's greatest weapon is a just cause that denies secrecy. There is no honor in hiding from your deeds.

If you do not own your intent, you will never find glory. However, if you face your foes, you know who they are and what led them to be your foe. Sometimes simply the act of facing your enemy can reveal that it is not your enemy you face.

MARTA AND THE SUITOR

One of the members of the Ketha royal family defeated by Ki'Var was the Lady Marta. When she was a youth, she was promised to be mated to General Yakan, a blood brother to Marta's father, the Great Kamlaq. But Kamlaq discovered that Marta had fallen in love with another, though Marta would not reveal the name of her illicit lover. Kamlaq assumed it to be Yakan's aide, Lieutenant Mavat.

Kamlaq confronted Mavat on the fields of his estate and accused him of dishonoring him with his actions. But Mavat had no idea what Kamlaq was talking about. When Kamlaq confronted Mavat, he saw only confusion in the young warrior's eyes. Kamlaq ordered Mavat bound by law until he could determine the truth of the matter. Eventually, Marta revealed her lover, a man who was not Mavat. The suitor committed *Mauk-to'Vor* to avoid disgrace. Marta was mated with Yakan, and they soon came to rule Ketha.

Had Kamlaq not challenged Mavat himself, had he struck without showing his face as Kranx did, he might well have ended the same way as Kranx. Instead, he confronted Mavat directly and avoided giving either himself or Mavat a dishonorable death.

When Yakan and Marta became the rulers of Ketha, Mavat served as their Chief Warrior. Theirs was a prosperous and honorable reign, and Mavat led their troops to many great victories, and only the one, final defeat at Ki'Var's hands.

Kamlaq's actions led to honor. Marta was not forced to go back on her childhood vow to mate with Yakan, and she and he became great rulers. Mavat was not dishonorably killed for another's indiscretion, and instead became Ketha's mightiest warrior. Even Marta's suitor was able to die with honor, through the act of *Mauk-to'Vor.*

If you do not show your face, then your fight has no meaning. If there is no meaning to it, you cannot take possession of your battle. If you do not take possession of your battle, then your battle is worthless. If your battle is worthless, what worth have you?

K'RATAK'S COMMENTARY

It is disheartening to look back at Klingon history and see that it is truly littered with cowards who have killed without showing their faces. Kranx is a legendary example, of course, but it hardly ends with him. Indeed, many of the most vilified names in history are of those associated with this hideous crime: Qorvak, L'Pragh, Vilik, Krit, Chang, Duras, and others it causes pain even to mention.

The very first *Dahar* Master was Biroq, who was given the honor by the Emperor Kaldon. Biroq led the conquest of the Samnatti of Ty'Gokor, the first world outside our home system to be brought under the flag of the Klingon Empire. Biroq's martial triumphs were many, including his single-handed defeat of the guards who defended the Samnatti oligarchs. After planting the Klingon flag on Ty'Gokor and declaring the Samnatti to be *jeghpu'wI'*, Emperor Kaldon announced that Biroq was a hero of the Empire. He said there was no rank that could adequately describe his place within the military, so the emperor created a new one, intending it to be unique, a title for Biroq alone. The emperor dubbed him a *Dahar* Master, an achiever of legendary status.

Biroq's chief aide was Qorvak. Many of the tales written about Biroq do not even mention Qorvak until the end of the story, when he commits the deed by which his name was unutterably besmirched. One night, while Biroq slept, Qorvak crept into the *Dahar* Master's bedchamber and slew him.

Scholars and clerics have recently discovered records showing just how much of Biroq's success was the result of campaigns actually planned by Qorvak. (The *wam* serpent, a *ramjep* bird in disguise!) This has done a great deal to explain the resentment that drove him to his despicable act. Many of the records—unearthed during excavations of sites on Ty'Gokor damaged by orbital bombardment from the Borg during their invasion of the Alpha Quadrant—indicated that Biroq and Qorvak worked as equals. Biroq was the more charismatic of the two, so he gave the orders and sang the songs and made the speeches that would rouse the troops to battle. Qorvak was the intellect, the tactician who formulated strategy. Because Biroq's actions were more public, he received the majority of the credit.

But it matters not, because—even with these new revelations—Qorvak has been reviled throughout our history as the slime devil who slew the first *Dahar* Master in his sleep. Whether he was the mind behind Biroq's campaigns, whether he was robbed of his due credit for the conquest of Ty'Gokor, is of no import. He killed without showing his face. Had he challenged Biroq for supremacy of their forces, had he challenged Emperor Kaldon for dishonoring him by giving Biroq the glory for work they had performed together, he would be remembered as a warrior who died in honorable combat. Instead, the name Qorvak is all but synonymous with *coward* among our people. In thrall to his rage or his vanity—or some other demon driving him—he squandered a shining jewel. He cast off the thing of most value to him, the good name that is the proper vessel for honor.

Qorvak was unable to learn the lesson of this precept, but others were more fortunate. When we first encountered the Romulan Empire, war was immediate. Our two nations clashed over the Narendra system, and while

we have been allied with the Romulans from time to time, they have been our enemies far more often. General Mav led the first campaign against the Romulans in orbit around Narendra VI.

One of his fleet captains, Commander L'Pragh, believed Mav a fool, engaging the Romulans as he did. No other foe the Empire had yet faced was as mighty as the Romulans, and L'Pragh believed they would be better cultivated as allies. General Mav condemned L'Pragh's contention. "We are Klingons," the general famously said, "and our destiny is conquest. Aliens' sole purpose is to serve as the obstacles that render our victories meaningful."

Realizing that he would never have the support of the other warriors if he challenged Mav directly, L'Pragh acted instead as Qorvak did, stabbing Mav while he slept. Unlike Qorvak, though, he was not caught in the act, and investigators were never able to determine who had killed the general. L'Pragh took over command of the fleet and attempted to negotiate a settlement with the Romulans. But the Romulan commander sabotaged the negotiations, setting off an explosive in the conference chamber where they were to meet. L'Pragh realized the error of his ways and led an attack on the Romulan fleet. The resultant victory was our first against the Romulans, and L'Pragh was hailed as a hero of the Empire.

He did not maintain that distinction for long, however, for the guilt of his cowardly actions in killing General Mav without showing his face caught up to him, and was compounded by the knowledge that Mav had been right and he wrong. (A pale honor still clung to L'Pragh, like a flickering flame to a wick. It was this stunted nobility his guilt attacked, and here his fortress was breached. Like rust eating away at a weak point in iron, L'Pragh's guilt ate away at his resolve.) After the defeat of the Romulans, L'Pragh was found in his cabin, having committed *Mauk-to'Vor,* beside a letter wherein he confessed to his actions. Emperor Budlesh was forced to condemn L'Pragh only a few days after honoring him. L'Pragh's arrogance in refusing to believe that his commanding officer was correct led to dishonorable actions and a tainted, battered victory. But because he learned this lesson, albeit too late for Mav, he was able to salvage his honor and that of his family by means of *Mauk-to'Vor.* He showed his face at the end, to his own waiting death, confronting his crime. It was this reckoning that restored to L'Pragh the honor he had discarded.

Emperor Budlesh himself was the victim of a foe he never saw wield the weapon that killed him and the perpetrator of a similar violation as well. Many had tried to defeat Budlesh, who, in addition to being a great leader, was one of our finest warriors. When his throne was challenged by the forces of the outlaw Worna, Budlesh himself led a cadre of warriors to the ruins of Tong Vey, where Worna's forces lay in wait.

In those times, the emperor designated an heir to succeed him when he died. Only occasionally was that heir a blood relative, though the emperor always made *R'uustai*[14] with his heir. Budlesh's mate was the Lady Vilik, who had been grooming Kalfar—her son from a previous mate—to be heir. But Budlesh kept refusing to name an heir, and Vilik grew impatient. Finally, Vilik took it upon herself to begin slowly poisoning the emperor's food, after which time Budlesh became ill. No healer in the Empire could determine what ailed Budlesh, and eventually he died. Only after his death was it revealed that Budlesh knew of his mate's treachery and had already named his nephew, Yorq, to be his heir. Budlesh loved Vilik and would not go against her wishes in life. Instead, he condemned himself to a dishonorable demise. Klingons who die by poison are dishonored, but those Klingons who led an honorable life before their demise still have a place in *Sto-Vo-Kor*. Budlesh knew he was being poisoned, and yet chose not to stop it. His killer may not have shown her face directly, but he knew who it was and did nothing.

But knowing, he also sowed the seeds for his murderer's own death, for he informed Yorq of the truth regarding Vilik. Yorq begged Budlesh to condemn her, but he would not.

Emperor Yorq's first action upon ascending to the throne was to condemn both Vilik and Kalfar to death for treason against his uncle. The very justice that Budlesh could not exact himself, but which he knew his nephew would provide. Love veiled his judgment and blunted his hunger for honor, leaving both emperor and empress with dishonorable deaths that brought them to *Gre'thor*, where they can mourn their debasement together.

Perhaps the most bizarre such assassination was that of Emperor Skolar. Skolar's reign was one of decadence and corruption. The noble Houses of the Empire were more concerned with the acquisition of wealth than with the conquest of worlds. The Empire did not expand, the resources we had were exploited beyond prudence. The House of Kuzyk, for example, proceeded to buy up as much land as they could on Praxis and to create an industrial complex that

---

14   Literally, "the bonding." This brings a person who is not a blood relative into a noble House.

mined Qo'noS's moon. The industrial boom that followed led to great prosperity for the House of Kuzyk—and those to whom they sold the raw material—and eventually to Praxis's destruction.

During this dark time, wealth was kept within a few noble Houses. While industry increased, wages decreased sharply. Lowborn Klingons were forced to work for low wages in appalling conditions, while their employers grew wealthier.

The Defense Force was not immune to the corruption. The lower ranks swelled, as conditions in the factories proved a powerful recruitment incentive. But among the officer class, promotions were given not on merit, but were distributed as recompense for bribes paid to the High Council.

Out of that chaos rose a group of Klingons who called themselves *vo'ruv'etlh*.[15] They wore masks and never identified themselves individually, but always simply called themselves *vo'ruv'etlh*. Disruptor technology had just been developed, and any *vo'ruv'etlh* in danger of capture would turn their disruptors on themselves at the highest setting, vaporizing their bodies instantly and leaving no evidence.

(There are those who argue that the development of energy weapons was responsible for the decadence of Skolar's regime, as combat became too simple, too easy, allowing unskilled fools to rise in the ranks, padding their list of battles won with victories achieved by the simple pushing of a button. Let Klingons heave blades and strike and thrust!)

Over the course of an entire turn, *vo'ruv'etlh* killed those they viewed as dishonorable, ranging from ship captains to generals to members of the High Council. They became folk heroes among the people, especially among those who starved while the upper classes gorged themselves. The military and the High Council wished them stopped, however, and vast resources were expended trying to find them. But with so many incompetents at the highest ranks of the Defense Force—Klingons who had been given what should be earned—it soon became clear that they would never be able to do so.

While the *vo'ruv'etlh* proceeded from noble motives, their methods were flawed. One does not stop dishonorable behavior by behaving dishonorably. Fire cannot extinguish fire; it only goads fire to greater heights. The final act of the *vo'ruv'etlh* was an assault on the Great Hall, in which they killed the emperor and the entire High Council. They too perished when the Imperial Guard moved in

---

15   The Sword of Justice.

to capture them. In the end, the entirety of *vo'ruv'etlh* was vaporized, reduced to atoms in the air of the Great Hall. Emperor Skolar was dead, as was his heir and all those who ruled under him on the High Council.

As bad as Skolar's reign was, it was as nothing compared to what happened next. With no emperor and no council, anarchy reigned as dozens of noble Houses, fleet captains, and generals vied for power. The chaos lasted three turns before Emperor Yorlak seized power. While Yorlak was able to regain some stability, it was a decade before the Empire was prosperous again.

The mistake the *vo'ruv'etlh* made was in not showing their faces, in not claiming their cause openly. To this day, no one knows who they were, which Houses they belonged to—if, indeed, they belonged to any House—or why they chose their dishonorable path. Instead, they discarded honor and refused to show their faces, making them no different from Skolar's corrupt minions. In the end, they wiped each other out, leading to one of the darkest times in our history.

While the age of emperors has ended and the High Council has taken over rule of the Empire, the chancellors who lead the High Council have not been immune to cowardly attacks. Chancellor M'Rek faced tremendous turmoil as many factions on the High Council plotted against him, especially because the council was divided on the subject of where the Empire should stand on the Earth-Romulan War, as well as the disposition of the smooth-headed *QuchHa'* (some were from noble Houses, and couldn't simply be made second-class citizens of the Empire). By the time that war between humans and Romulans ended, the council was completely sundered, with M'Rek finding himself beset on all sides by a council that could agree on only one thing: they disagreed with M'Rek.

Shortly after that, M'Rek became ill, and the High Council assumed their troubles were over. M'Rek named an Arbiter of Succession, and then he died. But his autopsy was performed by a Denobulan doctor, who discovered that the virus that killed him was artificially created. The Denobulan was able to trace the evidence to the creator of the virus: a physician named Krit, a son of Antaak, the doctor who created the Augment virus that led to the creation of the *QuchHa'*. Krit claimed it was out of revenge for the way his father was treated, but Antaak himself condemned his son, and Krit was put to death.

In truth, the Empire was better off without M'Rek by the time he died, but the dishonorable mode of killing him showed Krit to be a fool and his cause to be less than just. Rather than pursue an honorable course, Krit resorted to trickery and the secrecy of shadows, and he died in deserved disgrace.

One of the most woeful events in the Empire's history was the industrial accident that resulted in the destruction of Praxis, the inevitable result of the House of Kuzyk's ravaging of the satellite. The consequent loss of industry and lives was grievous enough, but the moon's loss also portended long-term damage to the homeworld itself. Chancellor Gorkon took the initiative in reaching out to the Federation, long our blood enemies, for aid, thus laying the groundwork for an alliance that stands to this day and remains a cornerstone of the political landscape of the Galaxy.

But there were many who disagreed with Gorkon playing peacemaker, and they conspired to have the chancellor assassinated. The actual weapons that slew Gorkon were Federation phasers wielded by humans in Starfleet uniforms. However, they were merely the cat's-paws of a cabal of Klingon and Federation traitors who did not wish the relationship between the two nations to change. The leader of these animals on the Klingon side was General Chang. One of our finest soldiers for many turns, whose statue had already been erected in the Hall of Warriors, Chang plotted to destroy Gorkon while pretending to be his friend and comrade. (Plotting! Pretending! Who could think a noble end could come from such a beginning?) The conspiracy Chang took part in was exposed by the crews of two Starfleet vessels, and Chang himself was killed in battle against those ships. While it was a good end, at least, it came at the expense of revealing the dishonor of his life. His statue was destroyed within a week of his death, and his name was added to the list of the dishonored dead. Had he challenged Gorkon like a Klingon—openly, boldly—Chang might still be remembered fondly by our people as an honorable man.

Two of our most famous chancellors, the two whose reigns were the longest, were Azetbur and K'mpec. They both died without their killers ever showing their faces. Indeed, to this day, we do not know who killed either of them.

The daughter of Gorkon, Azetbur supervised the rebuilding of the Empire in the years following the destruction of Praxis. For all his progressive ways, Gorkon named her his heir like the emperors of old, a tradition that had been abandoned with the passing of the monarchy. But even with her outdated manner of succession, the people and the High Council embraced Azetbur, in part due to the crisis facing the Empire, in part due to respect for her father. After several turns, however, and a recovery that took longer than hoped, Azetbur lost the love of the people and the support of the High Council. Reactionaries led by Councillor Kaarg fought her at every opportunity. Though she had reigned longer than anyone in Klingon history, she was eventually killed with an assassin's *qutluch*. Upon succeeding her, Kaarg proclaimed his first edict: no woman would ever again serve on the High Council in any capacity.

Many rumors have circulated as to who wielded the blade that ended Azetbur's reign, though most believe it to be an assassin hired by Kaarg. A report unearthed in the archives of a listening post in the Pheben system damaged during the Dominion War indicated that Ditagh—an ally of Kaarg's who succeeded him as chancellor—was responsible, but no proof of that was ever forthcoming.

K'mpec's time ruling the High Council was longer than Azetbur's. He ruled longer than anyone in the Empire's history, whether chancellor or emperor. But he was brought low by a poison that had no antidote.

Councillor Duras and a political agitator named Gowron vied for the chancellorship, and K'mpec died believing that one of them was responsible for killing him. K'mpec charged his Arbiter of Succession—unusually, a human from the Federation—with finding out which of the two was responsible. However, Duras was killed in a blood feud before the ritual could be completed, leaving Gowron as the last one standing. During Gowron's ascension to the chancellorship, the truth about the House of Duras was revealed: his father, Ja'rod, collaborated with the Romulans in destroying the Khitomer outpost, and he himself conspired to keep that truth from being revealed, framing another for the crime. It was never proven that he poisoned K'mpec, but it is fairly certain that he did, an action that led to his family's dishonor. They were stained not only by the acts of Ja'rod, which caused the death of thousands of Klingons at Khitomer, but also by Duras's culpability in covering up the crime. His sisters attempted a coup, trying to install Duras's bastard son as chancellor, also with Romulan aid, but that failed, and soon thereafter they died in ignominy as outlaws. A once-mighty House was brought down by one of its scion's decisions to kill in secret while keeping another's crimes buried. What foul fruit grows from trees planted by cowards!

This third precept does not apply only to soldiers and politicians, of course. In the city of Krennla on Qo'noS, two brothers owned a set of dwellings that they wished to demolish. The structures were old and decrepit, and the cost to repair them was prohibitive. Moreover, repairing them would only postpone the inevitable collapse of these ancient homes. The younger brother wished to tell the tenants that they needed to move out, and to assist them in finding new

homes before destroying and rebuilding. The older brother thought that to be too much trouble. He thought it better for the tenants simply to leave on their own. So he contrived several accidents that forced the people to move out and to have the buildings condemned as unsafe to live in. The younger brother was disgusted by his brother's actions and confronted his sibling. When the older brother proved unrepentant, the younger one had little recourse. The older brother's wishes were paramount, so the younger brother could not challenge him.

Instead, he reported the deception to the Imperial Guard. That left the older brother subject to the law, and he was imprisoned for his actions, crimes that had been forged in the secrecy of his heart. Then the younger brother faced the tenants and told them the truth. The people were resettled, the buildings destroyed, and new homes built. It was the sibling who acted honorably who benefitted, both materially, through the new homes, and spiritually, by confronting the situation rather than hiding in the shadows of anonymity.

An honorable Klingon enters to trumpets, announcing himself, and he bears his cause like a pennant. In the short term, it can often be easier to simply do as you please, to act without showing your face. Indeed, Qorvak, L'Pragh, Vilik, Krit, Chang, the *vo'ruv'etlh*, and Azetbur's and K'mpec's assassins all achieved their short-term goals. But in the long term, their ends were as poor as their means. Crooked birth, crooked death. What begins without honor ends the same. But Klingons of character do not concern themselves with questions of ease or difficulty. Just as a sword's quality is determined by its sharpness, its balance, its heft—and not by how light a burden it is—the rightness of an action is to be judged according to its nature, not by how easily it may be accomplished. A worthy cause can bear the weight your honor piles upon it.

Fourth Precept

Seek adversity.

"The hunt tempers a warrior and makes him stronger."

—Kahless

Animals act only to survive or to ensure the survival of their young. More than anything, an animal must live, and that need overrides everything else.

DICTUM: THE ARDUOUS PATH

WARRIORS MUST KEEP THEIR FEET ON THE ROAD TO STRIFE. HONOR CAN BE FOUND ALONG THE WAYSIDE, AN HONOR BORNE OF SACRIFICE. BEWARE THE PRIZE WON EASILY. IT IS A STONE HUNG AROUND YOUR NECK, AND IT TESTIFIES ONLY TO THE FACT OF ITS OWN IRRELEVANCE. COMFORT SUMMONS INDOLENCE, INACTION, AND INSIGNIFICANCE. TO SHRINK FROM DANGER IS TO SHRINK FROM DUTY. BUT RIGHTEOUSNESS DEMANDS MORE THAN HOLDING ONE'S GROUND. IT CALLS THE WARRIOR TO RUN INTO THE WHIRLWIND, FOR THIS IS WHERE GLORY DWELLS. LET STRUGGLE—NEVER PRUDENCE, NEVER WHAT IS MERELY REASONABLE—BE YOUR CRITERION, RIGOR YOUR LAW.

THE KRI'STAK MOUNTAINS

Kahless once spoke of two warriors who needed to travel across the Kri'stak Mountains to reach a battle. Two routes could take them there. One led through the valley. It would be an easy journey, but it would take an extra day. The other went through the Kri'stak woodlands, which would enable them to arrive faster, but it presented difficult terrain filled with vicious predators.

Few had travelled the Kri'stak woodlands and survived, and one warrior insisted on going through the valley. The other, though, knew they were needed and any delay was unacceptable.

Unable to come to terms, the warriors split up. One went through the valley, the other through the woodlands.

While traversing the forest, the warrior who had chosen the quicker but fraught route faced a herd of *klongats*, dozens of birds of prey, a nest of needle vipers, and lava swamps.

He had expected dangers, though not so many. No maps had warned him of the lava swamps, and no travelers' accounts warned him of the *klongats* and other predators living among the trees. He found himself surprised by each new obstacle that the woodlands placed in his path.

Because of those trials, his arrival at the battle was delayed so much that he reached it at the same time as his comrade who had taken the easier but longer route.

But the warrior who had marched through the woodlands was battle-ready, having prepared himself for combat through the foes he faced in the forest. The one who went through the valley was less prepared, due to the ease of his journey; he fell quickly in battle, while the other triumphed.

Adversity increases awareness. Danger opens one's eyes, enabling a warrior to truly see. Facing a foe makes one stronger.

There are times when a foe is not readily available. A warrior becomes a warrior through combat, it is true. But combat does not always present itself.

When there is no combat, you must seek out a substitute.

ON THE VIRTUES OF THE HUNT

One of the ways that warriors can hone their skills is by hunting. Not in the mere killing of beasts, for that is a simple skill, all the more so if the animals be in the cage of domesticity.

But there is a thrill, a danger, an honor in seeking out the beasts in their own element, hunting them down, and taking their lives.

In some ways, it is a form of combat. Just as battle with a fellow Klingon requires skills that must be developed over a lifetime, so too with hunting.

You must learn the terrain your prey travels in. You must learn how to move within that terrain, to comport yourself to it, so that the animals do not hear you coming and hide.

You must learn to determine the scent of the animal, and to sense the patterns of the wind so that you remain downwind of the animal and your prey cannot smell you coming and flee.

You must learn to wield a sword or spear or other blade with which to slay the animal when at last you catch up to it.

You must learn to expose yourself to danger. You must experience the heightened sensations that come only from living in jeopardy. While safety excels in wearing down warriors, danger and adversity are honor's whetstones. Scoured by strife, a Klingon shines. Affliction affirms the Klingon who dares.

The emphasis here is on learning. Hunting is a skill like any other, and it requires patience and understanding. While hunting is not the same as combat, the skills required are similar. Hunting is also a bridge built of failures, but one that will lead the way across, in time, to victory.

While one should indeed choose one's enemies well, sometimes none are provided. But the beasts of the wild are legion. One need only go into the woodlands of the homeworld to find *targ, khrun, klongat, lingta, trigak, tangqa'*, and more. All provide a challenge for any warrior.

And they enable you to bolster your battle skills. Animals are creatures of pure instinct. They act only to survive or to ensure the survival of their young. While they have no conception of honor or duty, they do have sharpened instincts. More than anything, an animal must survive, and that need overrides everything else.

A foe that values survival over all is the hardest foe to defeat.

THE MOK'BARA

Another method of refining one's battle skills when there is no foe is the *mok'bara*.

The origin of the art is lost to antiquity, but the *mok'bara* provides the basis for Klingon combat. At its most fundamental, the *mok'bara* teaches simple

forms. Precise arm, leg, and body movements help to strengthen the body and cleanse the spirit.

A warrior can learn many useful methods of combat through the forms of the *mok'bara*.

Beginners first learn the *way'gho* parry,[16] as well as the *toch majQa'* strike.[17] These movements are done slowly, with purity and focus, in order to build strength of technique. In the early stages, students also learn many stances, including *tlhop lol*,[18] *jen lol*,[19] *'eS lol*,[20] and *Hun lol*.[21]

More advanced techniques involve the correct manner of wielding the weapons of combat. Students who are ready for them begin with basic thrusts and parries with a short blade, such as a *d'k tahg*. From there, the student progresses to more complex maneuvers involving longer blades. First a *tik'leth*, then a *mek'leth*, then a *bat'leth*.

Eventually one progresses to the *chenmoH*,[22] which are complex combinations of maneuvers, stances, steps, parries, and strikes. Each is more complicated than the last, starting with *nap*,[23] which uses only *way'gho* and *toch majQa'*. Only those who achieve master status learn *chenmoH'Itlh*,[24] the most complex of the forms.

The repetition of these forms prepares one for combat. Performing the simplest movements and practicing the simple forms again and again makes one ready to engage them instinctively when confronted by a foe. The fist can remember what the mind forgets.

In the end, a foe is not necessary for a warrior to engage in combat. Enemies take many forms. Adversity is a foe to be approached, not avoided, and embraced wherever it can be found.

---

16   Circular parry.

17   Palm-heel strike.

18   Front stance, which involves leaning forward on one bent leg in front of you, while the other leg is angled and straight behind you.

19   High stance, where you stand on one leg, the other off the ground and braced behind the knee of the standing leg.

20   Low stance, where one foot is slightly in front of the other and both knees are bent so that you're almost crouching.

21   *Khrun* stance, where you stand very low with feet wide apart, imitating how one rides a *khrun*.

22   Form (the equivalent of a *kata* in Japanese martial arts on Earth).

23   Simple form.

24   Advanced form.

K'RATAK'S COMMENTARY

The fourth precept has always fascinated me the most, for a variety of reasons.

Hunting is a sacred Klingon rite, and has been for many turns, and most Klingons assume that it is one of many teachings passed on to us by Kahless. But Kahless, as best as can be determined, was not a hunter. None of the sacred texts—not even the hidden scrolls that were revealed to the public when the clone of Kahless appeared and became emperor—make a single mention of Kahless hunting, with one exception, that being the quote that goes with this precept. Even then, the quote is out of place in the greater context of that particular chapter in the sacred texts. Here is the full quote:

> **"A warrior may taste battle in more ways than one. The hunt tempers a warrior and makes him stronger. It also provides him with sustenance to feed him in time for battle. That is also why farmers are so valuable, for a warrior marches on his stomach as much as his feet."**

Kahless was speaking primarily about the need for food—not an irrelevant concern—but the author of *qeS'a'* thought it important enough to take that one sentence and make of it a precept involving something separate from what Kahless was speaking of.

But now, hunting has become a critical part of a highborn warrior's life. There isn't a noble House in the Empire without access to hunting grounds, if not on its own estate, then elsewhere. As stated in the quotation, it is a simple way to hone one's skills without having to wait for a foe to arrive. Indeed, it is easier than ever to hunt, for there are preserves throughout the Empire. Several worlds—Krios, Archanis, Qu'vat, No'mat, and many others besides—have huge hunting preserves, and there are hunting competitions throughout Klingon space every year. Still, unlike so many essential aspects of Klingon society and culture, we do *not* owe it to Kahless.

Perhaps that explains the infamous Councillor B'alikk, who served under Chancellor Kravokh and also Chancellor K'mpec. For many turns, he railed against the practice of hunting. He gave dozens of speeches in open council, in which he denigrated hunting as a barbaric and outdated practice. "We are not the uncivilized Klingons of old," he would say, "who needed to hunt in order to survive. Do not doubt the Empire, which provides food for its people without the need to engage in obsolete rituals."

However, every time he attempted to outlaw hunting, his proposal was shot down. In fact, only once did a councillor other than B'alikk vote yes on one of these resolutions, and that was a junior councillor who owed B'alikk a favor.

When K'mpec challenged Kravokh following the Khitomer massacre and defeated him, he ascended to the chancellorship. As soon as the next council session commenced, B'alikk proposed the outlawing of hunting once again, hoping a new chancellor would be more amenable to his arguments.

K'mpec wasn't, but he also knew that Kravokh's response to B'alikk—ignore him and hope he would go away—would not work, especially since he was gaining support among a group of militant scientists. K'mpec had another councillor casually ask B'alikk if he'd ever actually hunted.

B'alikk was aghast. "Of course not!" he shouted, recoiling as if struck. "I do not engage in primitive barbarism from the time when Klingons wore loincloths!"

When word of his response got back to K'mpec, the chancellor had the information he needed. He sent formal invitations to the councillors, inviting them to go hunting with him. Ostensibly, it was an opportunity for a new leader of the High Council to get to know the warriors he was leading in the political arena.

B'alikk tried to refuse the invitation. After all, he reasoned, K'mpec had served on the High Council for many turns before he challenged Kravokh. The only change to the council was the appointment of Qurrt to take his place. B'alikk and K'mpec already knew each other well.

Ultimately, however, B'alikk could not refuse a direct request from the supreme commander of the Empire. So he went to the imperial hunting grounds in Ketha Province and reluctantly joined K'mpec for a *lingta* hunt. The councillor himself described the experience in a lengthy speech he gave in open council, during which he made it clear that he would never introduce a resolution to outlaw hunting again. An excerpt from that speech:

"I went to Ketha with dread, endeavoring to focus primarily on the opportunity for a day's unfettered access to the chancellor and endeavoring *not* to think about the insanity of what we would be doing. I have lived all my life in the First City, where the odors are vile, or on space ships, where the atmosphere is regulated. This was my first time in a region of pure nature, and it was eye-opening—and nose-opening. The scents overwhelmed me at first, but also did much to get my blood boiling in a way it hadn't since my youth. The flowers, the bushes, the birds, the beasts—it all amazed and astounded me. And when I tracked down the *lingta* and slew it, I felt more alive than I had in many turns."

Just as combat is a crucible, so too is hunting. At its finest, the hunt dissolves away irrelevancies until it is just you, your prey, and the wind. B'alikk learned what should have been obvious to him by seeing for himself what the hunt entails. And he had the integrity to change his mind. A mind that cannot change is a door that cannot open: both are useless.

And then we have the *mok'bara*. The main reason why this precept has been of particular interest to me is due to my own *mok'bara* studies. As I write this I am preparing for the weeklong ordeal that will grant me—if I survive—master status in the *mok'bara*.[25]

Since *qeS'a'* was first published, scholars have been able to determine some of the origins of the *mok'bara*. Classes in the art were first taught by Koshi and his daughter, Gijin. Koshi lived on the island of Qirak'a, which later, decades before Kahless's birth, sank in a tectonic shift. But by that time, the art had spread to the entire world, thanks to the adherents of Koshi's and Gijin's tireless traveling.

It was an excavation on Qirak'a that unearthed documents telling us of Koshi and Gijin, including letters exchanged between father and daughter. Koshi said that the *mok'bara* "would bring focus and energy to warriors' techniques." Koshi focused primarily on combat, while Gijin was more interested in the enriching of the spirit.

"A warrior," Gijin wrote, "can learn techniques through the *mok'bara*, but what I find most valuable is that *anyone* may practice the forms. The elegance of the motions and the grace of the techniques are such that they can be taught to all." In fact, today there are *mok'bara* schools across the Empire, and many of them begin with teaching small children. Even a child may easily learn *nap chenmoH*, as can others who may not be of the warrior class, but who still wish to master the techniques of combat. As one advances, one learns more difficult techniques, of course.

Where combat is the embodiment of wild, intoxicating chaos, *mok'bara* brings order. In fact, that was what appealed to me when I first began studying. At the time, I was but a callow youth who had difficulty concentrating on anything. I was too uncoordinated for combat, too uninterested to focus on anything else. At their wits' end, my parents enrolled me in a *mok'bara* school, one in Kopf's Cliff taught by K'Dar, a master of the art. He recognized my youthful stubbornness

---

25   K'Ratak did, in fact, survive, and as of the printing of this volume has achieved master status.

and challenged me by declaring me unfit to take the class. Angered, I pushed myself to prove him wrong. For the first time in my young life, I found something to concentrate on. I was bound and determined to move on beyond *chu'wI'*.[26] That adversity shaped me. It was the anvil upon which I was beaten and molded. K'Dar knew that the wise teacher forces students to teach themselves.

But still, though I practiced, I could not master *way'yeb*.[27] It didn't seem like a difficult technique—K'Dar, of course, performed it effortlessly, and even students who began their studies after me mastered it even while I continued to struggle. It was one of a dozen defenses I had to be able to execute perfectly before I could go for *chu'wI'Hey*.[28]

Months went by, and four people who had begun their tutelage after me were granted *chu'wI'Hey* status while I remained a beginner. And so one day I stayed at the school after it closed and did nothing but practice *way'yeb* over and over and over again until I finally did it without flaw—and then I did it a hundred more times.

When I told K'Dar of this, he laughed heartily, and told me the story of Woliv, the master who had taught K'Dar's master the art. Woliv also had a technique he could not perfect, and so his teacher told him he could not advance. Irritated, Woliv went into the woods and proceeded to strike at the trees—one of the strikes he used was the one he hadn't mastered, and he used it to shatter the tree. It was a complete accident, and he tried to re-create what he did. When he finally did so, he then executed it a hundred more times—just as I had. Woliv called this *poHmey vatlh*.[29] K'Dar granted me *chu'wI'Hey* status right then and there, for I had learned a valuable lesson of the *mok'bara* without even knowing it.

I had sought adversity and become stronger for it. The focus I gained as a student of *mok'bara* is directly responsible for my ability to write, which in turn led to my career. In many ways, I owe everything in my life to the art—and to this precept, for had I not sought adversity, I would not be writing this commentary today.

I still teach *mok'bara* classes when my schedule permits it, at the same school where I trained. K'Dar still teaches as well, though he has grown old. They say old warriors are as rare as wise fools. K'Dar is one of the rare ones, then. He

---

26   Novice.

27   Wrist parry.

28   Advanced novice.

29   The hundred repetitions.

does not shy from battle, but—as one of his students, Captain Klay, command-er of the Tenth Fleet, put it—"He simply has yet to come across a foe worthy enough to send him to his death." One of the finest *mok'bara* masters in the Empire, he is seldom challenged, but due to his age, he is rarely able to teach a full slate of classes. Luckily, many of his grateful students, like me, happily step in.

About a year ago, there was one student who was incredibly difficult. The youth was recalcitrant, refusing to follow simple instructions, and he responded poorly to attempts at correction. Furthermore, he came with two bodyguards to every class. I quickly learned—because he announced it boldly—that his name was Torvol, and he was of the House of K'Tal, a family that has served on the High Council since the days of Chancellor Kravokh. His father was K'vel'kar, the owner of one of the premier *bat'leth* smithies in the Empire, his uncle was General Talak, and the head of his House of course served on the High Council. The warrior without a reputation borrows his family's. And a borrowed reputa-tion is a threadbare cloak. However, threadbare though Torvol's cloak may have been, it was enough to prevent me from properly disciplining him, which meant there was nothing I could teach him.

I asked K'Dar what the boy was doing in the class, and the master simply sighed. The House of K'Tal was not to be trifled with, and if K'vel'kar wished to enroll his son in the school "to make a warrior of him," then K'Dar was to try. My own opinion was that Torvol lacked the equipment for such a manufacture. In the last class I taught before I went on a lengthy voyage offworld, I told Torvol that he was wasting his time, that he would never master the *mok'bara* because the forms teach combat, and Torvol's upbringing had guaranteed that he would never see combat. As if to prove my point, his two bodyguards moved to stand between us. I turned my back on him and the bodyguards both. Later, I was told that K'Dar had to talk Torvol out of ordering my death.

I wouldn't have given the youth a second thought, but shortly after our encounter, his personal transport was ambushed by Kreel pirates. While Torvol survived, he lost his left arm in the attack. After he recovered, he returned to K'Dar's school just as I was there to teach a few classes. Although there were many forms he could not do, Torvol tried harder than anyone in the class, and mastered every form that he could in a remarkably short time. He even man-aged to get through *pa'Qaw' chenmoH*,[30] a difficult one to perform with only

---

30   Literally "destroy the castle." This form simulates a single warrior fighting all those who defend a mighty castle.

one arm, for it has many instances of *jen lol*, requiring balance that is hard to manage one-armed.

In his case, he had not sought out adversity, but rather it sought him out. The result was the same: he became stronger. Had he sought the adversity on his own by studying the *mok'bara* more thoroughly, he might have become a proper warrior on his own instead of the coddled scion of a noble House that shielded him from his weaknesses. But adversity was provided for him, thus at last permitting him the opportunity to overcome the weaknesses that had so crippled his honor. When K'vel'kar died, Torvol was able to take over the smithy.

Safety breeds weakness. Adversity creates strength.

Fifth Precept

Reveal your true self in combat.

"We do not fight merely to spill blood, but to enrich the spirit."

—Kahless

But B'Ennora looked at Volagh, who was not yet dead. They exchanged a glance, and B'Ennora knew instantly that Volagh was no traitor. Before Taklat could speak or attempt to conceal himself once more, she killed him.

DICTUM: THE SHATTERED MASK

WARRIORS MUST VENTURE INTO THE LABYRINTH. COMBAT IS THE WAY, AND AT THE CENTER IS THE SELF. DISCOVER AND DECLARE YOUR TRUEST SELF, THAT WHICH LINGERS WHEN EVERYTHING ELSE HAS BEEN STRIPPED AWAY. BEYOND VICTORY, BEYOND DEFEAT. BEYOND EVERY NEED AND THE SATISFACTION OF EVERY NEED. HAVING PASSED THROUGH THE WASTES, THE DESERTS SOWN WITH DEATH, YOU MUST HOLD YOUR BANNER HIGH AND UNFURL IT. THERE, ON THE BATTLEFIELD, SHATTER YOUR MASK, FOR IT SERVES AN OBSOLETE PURPOSE. BY YOUR WARRING, YOU HAVE ALREADY MADE YOURSELF PLAIN. A WARRIOR HAS NO MORE SECRETS.

STRENGTH FROM WEAKNESS

When two warriors come together in battle, it is not a time for sorrow, dismay, or fear, but for celebration.

Warriors are at their finest when they have a battle to fight, a cause to fight for, and a worthy foe to face.

The one certainty of life, the one thing that everyone, warrior to beggar, can count on is death. Death can be bought but never sold. For that reason, nothing is more important than how one faces death.

Simply waiting for death is foolish and dishonorable. Death will arrive regardless, so why wait? Embrace the inevitable. Seize it and bring death closer! No treasure was ever won by waiting.

Death is the one foe that everyone faces, the one foe that never loses. But to avoid the battle will only allow death to stab you in the back. Like any foe, death must be challenged and it must be battled. To do otherwise brings shame to the greatest battle of all, that of life.

The will required to do battle is tremendous. Not all are born with it, which is why we train, so we can achieve that will.

Once Kahless told the story of two children, a boy and a girl. The boy was already strong, and declared his intent to become a warrior. The girl was smaller and also younger, but she too wished to be a warrior. The boy laughed at the girl, saying she could never be as strong as him.

Years passed. The boy, knowing himself to be strong, did not bother to train, assuming that his strength would always carry the day. The girl, though, studied the *mok'bara*, played games of strategy, and tutored with a blade instructor. She remained physically frail, but she fought to overcome her weakness of body by the strength of her spirit. Battle is the finest teacher, and the girl was an apt pupil.

She met the boy again, and challenged him, *tik'leth* in hand. He laughed and mocked her sword, but unsheathed his own weapon. At first, the fight was one-sided, and the boy's strength was his advantage. He had no skill with the sword, so he attempted simply to club her with it. But the girl had been trained to use her smaller size and relative weakness as assets. The blind can still hear the truth of things, after all. So she dodged his blows, avoided his strength.

In the end, she defeated him. She moved in close, leaving him unable to benefit from his longer reach. She plunged her sword into his chest.

Kahless explained then that the body is just a physical shell. It is the heart that determines a warrior, and battle that determines the heart. A casual observer would believe the boy to be the fighter and the girl to be weak, but combat revealed the nature of their truest selves. One may never judge the sharpness of a blade by its sheath.

There are other methods of combat just as revealing, even where no weapons are raised.

KLIN ZHA

During his travels following his battle against Morath, Kahless journeyed from the First City to the distant peninsula of Kalranz. He wished to bring the laws of honor to the people there. In a park near the cliffs that overlooked the great ocean, Kahless saw a man and a woman playing a game with pieces on a board. He had never seen such a game before. He asked the players, who were mates named Kaprav and Vis'Ar, to explain it to him. They called it *klin zha*, which derives from very old Klingon, and it translates roughly as "the game of the people."

The game had eighteen stones, nine green, nine gold. Each stone could move in a different manner and each was maneuvered to capture a neutral piece, called the Goal. Kahless admired the game and immediately asked to be taught to play. He spent the entire day in that park, playing first Kaprav, then Vis'Ar.

Kaprav and Vis'Ar told Kahless they created the game as a method of refining one's combat strategies. They told him nobody had mastered the game as quickly as Kahless had, which indicated his wisdom.

Other games Kahless was familiar with test strength and accuracy. Many times, Kahless spoke of the times he played *B'aht Qul*[31] with his brother Morath when they were youths. That game has two warriors face each other across a table as each presses the back of his hand against other's. Whoever can push the other's hand to the table surface first wins.

From the moment they can pick up a spear, every Klingon child plays *Qeq ghIntaq*,[32] which measures aim.

However, Kahless realized that the true heart of a warrior can be found in *klin zha*. Only *klin zha* tests the mind of a warrior, the ability to strategize and anticipate one's foe's next move and to counteract it.

---

31   The origins of the name of this contest are in dispute. Some believe that it was created by a Klingon named B'aht Qul. Others believe it derives from a remote region where the dialect of the Klingon language has drifted considerably.

32   Literally, "aim the spear." The game has one player roll a hoop down an incline and the other player attempts to throw a *ghIntaq* spear through it cleanly without touching the edges of the hoop.

When he left Kalranz, Kahless brought a board and game pieces on his travels. He taught the game to everyone he knew. He met with many warlords, kings, tyrants, and warriors. Some flew to his banner right away. Others resisted. All of them were challenged to a game of *klin zha*.

The leader of the island nation of Kall'ta did not believe that Kahless's cause was just, but he did accept the challenge of a game. His strategies were simplistic, he did not think past the current move, and Kahless defeated him easily every time. Kahless knew he would be easily conquered. His armies accomplished that task within a month.

Another warlord, this one from the mountains of Pak'thar, felt the same as the Kall'ta leader. But he played *klin zha* with verve and brilliance, defeating Kahless as often as Kahless bested him. This was a foe who would be difficult to challenge, so Kahless let him be until his own position was stronger. Months later, the lands surrounding Pak'thar had all adopted Kahless's banner, and the warlord pledged himself to Kahless as well.

When that warlord did so, he told Kahless that he admired the strategy, as it was very much like a *klin zha* maneuver. If you cannot take the Goal, occupy the territory surrounding it. The Goal will eventually fall to you.

Games of strategy reveal much about a warrior's heart. Not only do they reveal how a warrior reasons, but also the tactics the reasoning will devise. Two warriors may target the same goal but acquire it differently. *Klin zha* helps show the differences and similarities among warriors. It shows them their own paths to victory.

TO GRIP A WEAPON

Another manner in which a warrior's true face can be revealed is in the holding of a weapon. One of Kahless's followers was the great warrior Amar, who trained warriors in the use of the *bat'leth*, the mighty sword that Kahless first forged.

Amar once famously said he could tell the quality of a warrior simply by the manner in which the *bat'leth* was held. If you held the blade against your shoulder, grip facing outward, Amar had little faith that you were a good warrior. It would take too long to move the weapon into a defensive position, requiring its bearer to grab it and turn it around. Also, if you hold the weapon that way, your grip puts the blade against your body. A foe could wound you by simply pushing against the *bat'leth*.

Even holding it in that same position but with the blade held outward and the grip against your shoulder, you still prove yourself more interested in how you look than in how you fight.

A true warrior cares more for readiness than appearances. A black *trigak* kills as surely as a white. Warriors trained by Amar always knew to hold the *bat'leth* either cradled in the crook of the arm with one hand on the far grip, or in a two-handed grip at an angle in front of them.

Those who hold their weapons ready to fight assure their foes that they can.

VARGO AS A YOUTH

Combat also reveals one's own true self to oneself.

After Vargo, the warlord who ruled the Tenka Plains, pledged his allegiance to Kahless, he told the story of how he came to power.

When he was still but a youth, his parents were killed in an accident, trampled by a *khrun*. Vargo was too young to rule, but his father's chief advisor, Kimrek, served as his regent. Kimrek convinced Vargo he was too sickly to be a warlord, that he had neither the head nor the heart for it. Eventually Vargo conceded most of the power to him, while he tried and failed to improve his health.

Not long after, a plague ravaged the region. Vargo visited many of the sick as they lay dying. One of them was an old woman who apologized to Vargo. As she expired, she confessed to Vargo that she had poisoned the *khrun* that trampled his parents, deranging it.

Her last words named Kimrek as the person who hired her.

Vargo's fury was amazing to behold. Despite his illness, he took up arms and challenged Kimrek. Though Kimrek was a great warrior, Vargo had righteous outrage on his side.

The two of them fought for most of a day. Despite his illness, despite his lack of training, Vargo was able, eventually, to defeat Kimrek and stand alone as warlord of the Tenka Plains.

Later Vargo learned that Kimrek had also been slowly poisoning *him*. The sickly nature that Kimrek had used as a pretext for taking power was in fact of his own creation. In challenging Kimrek, Vargo found himself at last, and he ruled Tenka for the rest of his days.

Nothing reveals a warrior spirit more than the act of combat itself. Whether on the *klin zha* board or on the battlefield or in the noble rage of the duel, the act of battle rouses the spirit and reveals the warrior's true face.

K'RATAK'S COMMENTARY

Ty'Gokor has always been a fortress of the Empire. One of the best-defended worlds in Klingon space, it is the site of the inductions into the Order of the *Bat'leth*[33] and the headquarters of many sections of the Defense Force and Imperial Intelligence. It was also the temporary capital of the Empire after Qo'noS was devastated by the Borg.

This stronghold of a planet—long enjoying a reputation as the most secure world in the Empire—was breached only once in our history. It appeared to be a Romulan attack, made shortly before the Tomed Incident that led to that empire closing its borders. In reality, it was a betrayal by the House of Taklat. That House, as stated in an earlier commentary, had fallen into financial ruin after the destruction of Praxis, and was indebted to several Romulan nobles, who made loans to House of Taklat to keep it alive. But the repayment of those loans came in the form of favors for the Romulan Empire. Many Houses did likewise after Praxis, leading to many attempts by the Romulans to take over the Empire covertly through these economic entanglements.

Taklat himself had come to Ty'Gokor, ostensibly to supervise the construction of a new base for the Defense Force on the island of K'velera, but in truth he came to sabotage the existing base for his Romulan masters, so they could attack. Under a cover of inspecting the generators—they would need to be duplicated in the new base—Taklat shot Lieutenant Volagh, the operations chief of the base, in the back, then brought the shields down. Commander B'Ennora, the leader of the base, went to the generator room to investigate the shields. There she found Taklat, who claimed to be trying to restore the base's defenses, and Volagh. Taklat alleged that Volagh had betrayed them.

But B'Ennora looked at Volagh, who was not yet dead. They exchanged a glance, a moment of *tova'dok*. They spoke without words, and B'Ennora knew instantly that Volagh was no traitor. She saw his true face in that moment, as well as Taklat's. Unsheathing her *d'k tahg*, she turned to Taklat. Before he could speak or attempt to conceal his true self once more, she killed him and restored the shields. Ty'Gokor remained safe until reinforcements could arrive.

---

33   The Order was formed by Lukara after Kahless's ascension, and the original purpose of its membership was to ensure that Kahless's teachings endured. The Order became largely ceremonial as the centuries wore on. However, following the Dominion War, Chancellor Martok returned the Order to its original purpose.

There is no discussion of *tova'dok* in *qeS'a'*, even though it is a notion that predates Kahless. It's one of those nebulous concepts that warriors either swear by utterly or refuse to believe in. *Tova'dok* is one of the ways warriors show their true faces to other warriors and prove who they are and what they are worth as honorable Klingons.

In the days before the Dominion War, Martok and Worf were imprisoned by the Dominion. As part of their imprisonment, they were put into a ring and forced to fight the Jem'Hadar. This was a method of training the soldiers of the Dominion to fight species from the Alpha Quadrant. After many rounds in the ring, Worf was close to giving up, ready to let the Jem'Hadar simply kill him rather than endure more torment. Imagine what anguish and pain the Jem'Hadar must have heaped on Worf's back to bring him to the brink of that, the darkest choice.

But then he and Martok looked at each other. Still a general at the time, the future chancellor stared into Worf's eyes and saw that the latter was prepared to die. Ashamed at his cowardice, Worf instead took strength from Martok and chose to continue fighting. Both Martok and Worf, who told the story to his former Starfleet commanding officer, Captain Benjamin Sisko, and to Giancarlo Wu, who served as his aide when he was Federation Ambassador to the Klingon Empire, described this moment of *tova'dok*. In the end, their shared moment revealed Worf's true face to himself, and he knew he had to change it or die in shame. It saved Worf's life and his honor. It was likely what led to his welcome into the House of Martok, of which Worf remains a proud member.

More fundamental than *tova'dok*, however, is the pith of the precept, that a warrior's true nature comes out in combat. Battle is difficult and arduous. For all the talk of ours being a warrior culture, we aren't all truly warriors. The elite are warriors, yes, and warriors are the elite. We elevate warriors to such status for a number of reasons, not the least being that becoming a warrior is a monumentally difficult proposition. The requirements are many: a warrior must be fit, must be swift, must be strong, must be smart, and must be cunning.

Warriors train from the moment they can first wield a blade, and the training never ceases. It is a true expression of one's capabilities, because there is no artifice when one fights. One can occasionally fool an opponent, and even sometimes oneself, but ultimately it is only one's skill, one's spirit, one's honor that will bring triumph.

One of the tests that teachers of *mok'bara* give to their students is *Daq*[34]. For this test, which is required in order to advance in rank, teacher and student face each other without moving. Whoever moves first is the winner—unless the move is too slow. It is a test of will, of discipline, of patience. Some *mok'bara* practitioners have stood facing each other for days on end before one finally made a movement. My own *mok'bara* master tells the story of the great teacher Woliv and his first *Daq* test with his teacher, Qey'cho. Qey'cho was a hard master, and very few students advanced under his tutelage. Woliv was the first person he had invited to take the *Daq* in fifty turns.

The test was held in the midst of the *qaDrav*[35] in the First City. Though that special place was generally reserved for combat between two warriors settling a disagreement, Qey'cho's reputation was such that he was given dispensation by the High Council to hold a *Daq* there.

People from *kellicams*[36] around came to see the test. Woliv and Qey'cho faced each other in the *qaDrav*, without moving, for minutes, hours, days. Spectators came and went, and the two warriors continued to face each other.

Qey'cho was no longer a young warrior by this time, and at one point— after facing his student for almost two full days—his left leg began to cramp. Even so, he did not move, but eventually he was forced to shift his footing or risk falling over completely. Woliv saw this shift, minuscule though it was, and moved quickly, striking with a low kick to his opponent's weakened leg. Qey'cho fell to the ground, and then laughed heartily, saying he had finally found a true warrior. He had suspected that Woliv was destined to be a *mok'bara* master, and this *Daq* had shown that to be his true destiny. It was through the *Daq* that Woliv announced himself. Qey'cho's first movement was small, simply a shifting of weight, but that was all Woliv needed to strike.

To know themselves, warriors must fight. Without battle, warriors' hearts remain secret, their true natures masked. Combat unfurls the banner of a warrior's spirit.

---

34   Literally, "against" or "versus."

35   Challenge floor.

36   A unit of measurement roughly equivalent to two kilometers, or one and a quarter miles.

Sixth Precept
Destroy weakness.

*"All Klingons have weaknesses. Warriors know to
hunt their weaknesses and cut them out."*

—Kahless

Faced with an Empire at its nadir, an Empire experiencing its worst moment since the Hur'q
invasion, Azetbur destroyed the weakness her opponents accused her of nurturing.

DICTUM: THE ENDLESS VIGIL

WARRIORS MUST WATCH WITH VIGILANCE. A WARRIOR'S FIRST QUARRY IS WITHIN: FRAILTIES OF SPIRIT, FLAWS THAT GNAW AT RESOLVE. THESE ARE MORE TREACHEROUS THAN A DECEITFUL FRIEND, MORE WOUNDING THAN A MATE'S BETRAYAL. YOUR WEAKNESS IS MORE POWERFUL THAN YOUR ENEMY'S STRENGTH. AT THE CRUX OF DANGER, WEAKNESS EMERGES FROM THE HEART, LIKE A BEAST FROM ITS LAIR. YOUR WEAKNESSES WILL CHOKE YOUR COURAGE, BLIND YOUR VALOR, AND SMOTHER YOUR WILL WHILE IT SLEEPS. HARDEN YOUR HEART AND MAKE IT LIKE THE STONY GROUND, INHOSPITABLE TO WEAKNESS. STALK WEAKNESS TIRELESSLY. SLAY IT WITHOUT MERCY. DISHONOR COMES NOT FROM WEAKNESS, BUT FROM SHELTERING WEAKNESS AND LOOKING ON WHILE IT MULTIPLIES, WHICH IT WILL, ALWAYS.

THE WARRIOR WITH ONE EYE

Only a fool claims to have no weaknesses, no vulnerabilities, no fear. Only fear demands fearlessness. It is for the warrior to find weaknesses and battle them. Weakness is simply another enemy for a warrior to face and eventually defeat, even though the foe be oneself. The skills a warrior develops in fighting external opponents may also be used to conquer those within. One axe will fell many trees.

Kahless witnessed a fight between two warriors who both desired the same woman for a mate. They fought for most of a day, and when night fell, the warriors each struck a brutal blow. One slashed the other in the eye, destroying it. Before collapsing to the ground, the blinded warrior thrust his sword into the other's shoulder, injuring him gravely.

In the end, neither warrior won the woman, as she chose another for her mate. Diminished, and shamed by their diminishment, the warriors wondered how to proceed.

The one whose arm was now useless chose *Mauk-to'Vor*. He did not feel he could be a warrior with only one arm. Kahless himself performed the ritual for him.

The one who lost his eye took a different view. Yes, he was a lesser warrior than his two-eyed comrades. However, he approached this as a challenge to overcome, not as a defeat to be mastered by. Kahless congratulated him and wished him well.

For many months, the one-eyed warrior trained. He told his training partners to attack him from his blind side, where defense would be more difficult.

By the time Kahless met the warrior again, a full turn had passed. Kahless challenged him to a friendly duel. Many times, Kahless did him the honor of attacking him on his blind side, and every time the warrior deflected the attack. Kahless was impressed.

Defeat spurs the wise warrior to new victories.

THE WISH TO REMAIN

The greatest defeat Klingons have ever suffered revealed a nearly crippling weakness within us. It was our first contact with beings from other worlds. It was the Hur'q invasion.

Kahless had united our people, ascending at last to *Sto-Vo-Kor*. He left behind only his *bat'leth*, the mighty Sword of Kahless. But then the Hur'q came and destroyed our cities, slaughtered our armies, plundered our possessions. They took the Sword of Kahless. They left us a defeated people. Conquered. Bereft.

It would have been easy for us to withdraw into our world, to warm ourselves at defeat's lowly fire. We could have remained on Qo'noS. Though death claims all Klingons in time, our world endures. There were many who claimed we should not leave the homeworld for that very reason. Space was filled with strange beings like the Hur'q. They would only bring death and destruction to Klingons. The demon at home is half as strong as the demon beyond, they said.

If we remained on our world, we would be safe. We would endure as Qo'noS endures, by remaining alone, sheltered from unknown dangers.

The wish to stay on Qo'noS was our weakness, and it needed to be destroyed.

KAHLESS'S PROMISE

Before he departed for *Sto-Vo-Kor*, Kahless made a promise. He said his work was done. The people wept, for they did not wish him to go. One person said, "We need you, Kahless!" Then Kahless turned to face them. "You are Klingons," he said. "You need no one but yourselves. I will go now to *Sto-Vo-Kor*, but I promise one day I will return." He pointed to the night sky. "Look for me there, on that point of light."

Debate raged among our people for months.

Some argued that Kahless's words meant we should stay on our world. Because he said we need no one but ourselves, some believed that we should avoid contact with aliens.

Others believed that Kahless was explicitly telling us to go into space, because he would return to another world.

And still others thought we should go to space for the simple reason that it was the only way to get the revenge upon the Hur'q that was our due.

CH'GRAN AND THE FLEET

It was the great warrior Ch'gran who led the charge. To remain on the homeworld wearing the rags of the conquered was cowardly. Only victory can mend a broken sword. To recover from our defeat required triumph in battle. And so Ch'gran oversaw the construction of mighty vessels that would take our people into the black sky. His seven ships left Qo'noS to conquer the Galaxy.

When Ch'gran acted, we vanquished the weakness that was our desire to be safe. Because of that, when we faced another defeat, we were ready. Ch'gran's fleet was lost, never to be seen again. However, Ch'gran's deeds inspired Klingons to build more ships. A new, more powerful fleet left Qo'noS to make other worlds tremble. Out there, beyond, we found the resources to rebuild what the Hur'q had destroyed.

Klingons need no one but themselves.

Our empire grows stronger every day because we have destroyed weakness in ourselves.

K'Ratak's commentary

Centuries later, even after crushing defeats at the hands of the Dominion and the Borg, it's safe to say that the most devastating loss in our history remains the Hur'q invasion. It was truly a turning point for our people, the moment that defined whether we would found a great empire, becoming a major power on the galactic stage, or remain a single planet of warriors unknown to the rest of the universe.

The decision that enabled us to destroy that weakness was ultimately made by Ch'gran. Startlingly, it was revealed only a few decades ago—when the Ch'gran wreckage was found on Raknal V near the Betreka Nebula—that Ch'gran created the space fleet not to seize new opportunities for conquest off Qo'noS, but only to make a weapon with which to conquer the homeworld itself, thereby supplanting the emperor. However, his first officer mutinied, and Ch'gran's fleet was lost. That officer's refusal to follow a murderous leader saved the Empire from Ch'gran's treachery.

Though Ch'gran proved to be a traitor to our people, his actions still spurred Klingons into leaping outward. Many of those who went with him did so not because they were complicit in his scheme, but because they truly believed in the ostensible purpose of the fleet. Indeed, that is why the mutiny succeeded and why Ch'gran's secret purpose came to naught. With enough noble followers, even a foul leader's goal is ennobled.

Perhaps the most important element of this particular precept is the way it's phrased: destroy not *your* weakness, implying a singular vulnerability that must be excised, but all weaknesses in general, wherever they can be found. Like stripes on a *trigak's* pelt, there is never only one. Indeed, the example of Ch'gran is telling, because even as he destroyed one weakness—some Klingons' cowardice in believing that the Hur'q invasion was a reason to stay isolated—he let another weakness fester: his own desire for power, no matter the deceit necessary to obtain it. Is ambition weakness? Is the impulse to conquer weakness? The desire to show strength and resolve and purpose? No, it is not these drives that are weak. In Ch'gran's case, it was his inability to resist the deceit, and the dishonor that accompanied it, that weakened him. He was overcome, paralyzed by it. He became a puppet to his ambition, and not the leader of his own cause, a saddled beast rather than a resolute rider. He surrendered his authority to an implacable hunger within him. That was his weakness.

Still, without Ch'gran leading us into space, we would never have reached Boreth, a world orbiting the star that Kahless pointed to in the Story of the Promise. The clerics continue to await Kahless's return there. Boreth was also where the clone of Kahless was created and made emperor. The expansion of our empire happened only because we wiped out the blight of the Hur'q invasion and turned a defeat into a victory.

Perhaps the figure in Klingon history with the greatest weakness to overcome was Azetbur. There are those who would argue that being female is not a weakness; others who would swear it is. Regardless, until Azetbur, no woman had ever ruled the Empire. Even the Lady Lukara took a subordinate position to Kahless, and she did not rule after his ascension (though she did much to preserve his legacy after he died). But after Chancellor Gorkon was assassinated, Azetbur took on his role. The first stroke makes the deepest cut. Pioneers win glory but pay dearly for it.

The destruction of Praxis had left the Empire in disarray, with Gorkon's subsequent assassination only worsening the situation. The Federation, long one of our most tenacious foes, offered assistance. Many in the Empire thought Azetbur a fool to accept any aid from our foes. One councillor quoted the old saying, "Better to starve than live on crumbs." But in truth, the Empire would not have survived without that help. Most estimated that Qo'noS would be uninhabitable inside of fifty turns without aid from outside. Azetbur's opponents threw Kahless's words back in her face: Klingons need no one but themselves. Many quoted another saying that predates Kahless: Drink not with the enemy.

Of course, Kahless hardly could have anticipated so catastrophic an event as the destruction of a moon, which was how Azetbur responded to those who criticized her. She did at least have the backing of several noble Houses, who suffered greatly from the destruction of Praxis. This made up for the inconsistent support of the military. After all, General Chang was one of the conspirators

behind Gorkon's assassination, and he attempted to do the same to Azetbur at the Khitomer Conference, all to prevent the very alliance with the Federation that she pioneered in her father's name. Even though Chang died in disgrace, many in the Defense Force supported his actions and his desire to keep the Empire from accepting aid from an enemy.

Faced with an Empire at its nadir, an Empire experiencing its worst moment since the Hur'q invasion, Azetbur destroyed the weakness her opponents accused her of nurturing. For her actions resulted in the alliance with the Federation that has become a cornerstone of the Galaxy. The alliance that led to the greatest era of prosperity in the Empire's history! The alliance that led to our victory against the Dominion! Azetbur saw what her critics could not: opening a door requires as much strength as closing it.

Sometimes the challenge is to discover what the weakness actually *is*. Discovering one's own vulnerability can be the greatest test a warrior faces. When he was in command of the *I.K.S. Gr'oth*, the *Dahar* Master Koloth was often challenged by Kuro, the Klingon who captained the legendary pirate ship *Taal*.

Kuro attacked worlds throughout the Empire. There was no pattern to his attacks, and no one ever knew where the *Taal* would strike next. His was the path of the *glob* fly, impossible to predict and just as impossible to ignore. After several attempts were made to track him down, Koloth was assigned the task. The two engaged in several firefights, with the *Taal* coming out the victor every time. Kuro, though, always stopped short of destroying the *Gr'oth*, claiming that he was a thief, not a killer. Koloth's response when Kuro's words came back to him was to sneer and quote an old aphorism: "Said the liar to the cheats, 'At least I'm not the worst of us.'"

For many turns, Kuro vexed Koloth, always attacking a place near the *Gr'oth*'s patrol sector, to make sure that it was Koloth who was sent after him. Kuro loved to torment Koloth, relishing his victories over the captain.

Every defeat, every escape that Kuro made, only angered Koloth further. The worst moment came after Kuro raided the colony on N'Vak. Koloth neglected to cloak his ship, resulting in heavy damage by the *Taal* the moment the *Gr'oth* came out of warp.

After N'Vak, Koloth realized that he was allowing his anger to get the better of him. Most Klingons view anger as a useful tool—indeed, for many of us, it is a constant state, for an angry warrior can be a mighty one. Anger, as they say, is the most useful muscle. But Koloth's anger was proving to be a detriment. Like fire, anger can be a tool, but like fire, anger can consume whatever it touches. Fire and anger both must be tamed. Koloth's anger was consuming his mind, his mettle, and it needed to be brought under control lest it destroy him with foolish strategies and poor judgment.

And so he eliminated it. He forced himself not to be reactive and angry, but measured and calm. He showed patience, combing through sensor logs and reports from all over the Empire. He even read through the after-action reports of his own warriors, forcing himself to relive his failed campaigns against the pirate, yet refusing to let his anger off its leash.

Eventually, Koloth was able to determine the location of one of Kuro's bolt-holes. He immediately set a course for that location—but Kuro was not there. So Koloth waited, remaining cloaked in orbit around the bolt-hole for many days on end.

When at last the *Taal* appeared in the system, Koloth engaged him in combat on his terms, not on those set by Kuro. Koloth destroyed the *Taal* and he achieved a great victory. The reputation that the *Dahar* Master would later have for ice water running through his veins was borne of his victory over the pirate. Koloth eliminated a flaw in his character; as a result, none but historians remember Kuro, except as one of the many defeated by Koloth, while Koloth himself is revered as one of the greatest warriors in the Empire.

[*Translator's note: K'Ratak's commentary on this precept also included a discussion of the Augment virus that produced a subset of Klingons with smooth foreheads. Indeed, the fact that this virus even existed is not common knowledge today. I was only able to find evidence of it in very old Federation records, from encounters with the Klingon Empire in the twenty-third century. Apparently, for the better part of a century, there was an entire subset of Klingons who had smooth foreheads, and looked very much like humans. That virus was cured in the late twenty-third century—so there's your destroyed weakness. These smooth-headed Klingons were physically weaker than their ridge-headed counterparts, and it was likely a great day for the Empire when the virus was finally cured, and all Klingons were as one again. Such an interpretation would certainly seem to fit with this precept. But I found only a single reference to the source of the virus, in the captain's and medical officer's logs of an old Earth ship from the mid-twenty-second century, which were light on details. The Klingon Information Net had nothing on it, and furthermore, the High Council refused to allow that portion of the manuscript to be included in this translation. When asked for a reason, their answer was simply, "We do not discuss it with outsiders."*]

SEVENTH PRECEPT

LEAVE NOTHING UNTIL TOMORROW.

"Battle delayed is battle lost."

—KAHLESS

While General Chu'paq waited for the right moment, Molor struck quickly, bringing his forces directly from Ketha to Kilgore Island. Molor slew Chu'paq himself, and now the tyrant was at last a sea power as well as a land power.

DICTUM: THE HIDDEN SERPENT

WARRIORS MUST KILL THE SNAKES THAT LIE IN WAIT. THESE ARE THE TASKS LEFT UNFINISHED, THE CHALLENGES LEFT UNMET. IGNORED, THEY GROW. FORGOTTEN, THEY ATTACK. THEY LURK AND WAIT TO SEIZE THEIR CHANCE. WHAT WARRIORS BEGIN, THEY MUST FINISH. HALF DONE IS UNDONE. EVERY PROBLEM WITHOUT A RESOLUTION—EVERY QUESTION WITHOUT ITS ANSWER—IS A DEBT IN LIFE'S LEDGER, A DEBT THAT BECOMES GREATER THE LONGER IT REMAINS. A WARRIOR'S DRIVE TO REACH THE END OF EVERY BATTLE MUST BE UNFLINCHING, FOR EVERY GOAL NOT YET ACHIEVED IS ABOMINABLE. KILL THE SERPENTS THAT WOULD KILL YOU FIRST.

THE LESSON OF AMAR

The first thing the great warrior Amar taught when he gave lessons in the use of the *bat'leth* was that the weapon should not be drawn except to be used.

If you are wielding a weapon, there is nothing to be gained by not striking with it. To draw a weapon and not use it dishonors the weapon, its lineage, its maker, and all who have come before you. Your weapon is not inert matter like a stone, or even a tool, like a mallet. It is an extension of yourself.

This is even more true of the *bat'leth*, Kahless's gift to all Klingons. To draw it and not let it serve you is to demean the gift and its giver.

It also gives your enemy a chance to strike first, an advantage you must not concede.

An action once committed to must be completed. Half a *khrun* cannot be ridden. The enemy you would kill tomorrow might attack you tonight. Any action that is worth taking is worth taking now.

To leave a task unfinished invites unwelcome circumstance and renders the task's completion less likely. Ask the family whose roof will be mended later how they like the damp.

THE TYRANT'S SON

There are many on Qo'noS who lived under Molor's tyranny. The lands in his grasp spread as far as the eye could see, and farther still. The entirety of the continent of Kastad was under his rule, as were many of the islands in the seas surrounding Kastad.

There was one island that refused to bend its knee to Molor, however. The island of Kilgore was located in the midst of the Chu'paq Sea, which was named for a general who served under Kilgore and won many campaigns for the warlord. The mountain at the island's center, Kilgore named for his mate, B'Elarana.

When Kilgore died of infection, his son, Yorif, became warlord. Nothing was ever named for Yorif, no sea, no mountain, no promontory. His only legacy was his parentage.

Chu'paq knew that the son was not the equal of the father and should be removed, but he bided his time. A fool does not stay a fool in secret for long. Chu'paq waited until Yorif's idiocy was no longer known only to those who had met him. He neglected the island's bridges, roads, and other structures, leaving them in disrepair. And though there is honor in building and rebuilding, in planning and erecting great structures, there is none to be found in dying while crossing a crumbling bridge.

Yorif instead spent the island's treasury on frivolity. He purchased works of art and then declared them hideous and hid them away. He hired singers and dancers and then refused to let them perform, though he would still pay for their services. And he employed chefs from all over the island to prepare massive feasts, and then proclaim himself not hungry and have the food disposed of.

Seeing the appalling waste, Chu'paq tried to convince Yorif that he needed to pay less attention to himself and more to those whom he ruled. But Yorif dismissed Chu'paq's words as inconsequential.

It was then that Chu'paq knew Yorif had to die. But Yorif was still the son of Kilgore, and the people still thought well of him.

As time passed, however, the people grew more and more disaffected with Yorif. Again, Chu'paq tried to convince Yorif of the wrongness of his course. Again, those words were dismissed.

With words denied a second time, Chu'paq was left only with actions. He challenged Yorif to honorable combat. Each was armed with a *Qingheb*,[37] and they faced one another on the island's sandy beachhead.

As the battle progressed, the entire island was calling for the general's victory. The last words Yorif heard were his subjects cheering his death.

Chu'paq believed patience led to his victory over Yorif. But the son of Kilgore would still have died a fool if the general had killed him instantly instead of waiting for him to drive Kilgore to ruin. Chu'paq would soon learn that his patience was an anchor dragging him to the depths.

Kahless's teachings of the need for honor and duty were taking hold throughout Molor's lands. His words inspired a rebellion in the Ketha region. Molor was forced to divert many of his troops to try to put down the rebels.

As the uprising in Ketha raged, Kahless and Lukara traveled to Kilgore. They pled with Chu'paq, telling him that Molor's flank was exposed. If Chu'paq's navy struck the coastline, the general would claim an important victory.

General Chu'paq refused. He did not believe the Ketha rebels would be able to hold off Molor's armies for very long, and while Chu'paq agreed that the coastline would be a prize handily won, holding it would prove difficult.

---

37   The *Qingheb* is an ancient weapon similar to a *ghIntaq* spear, but with a longer haft, a much larger and wider blade atop it, and a downward-curved horn protruding from the bottom of the blade. The *Qingheb* is rarely used anymore.

Chu'paq acknowledged the rightness of Kahless's cause. But patience, he thought—waiting for Yorif to ensure his own defeat—had gained him his throne, and patience would serve him well again. If a stratagem works once, he told Kahless and Lukara, it will work again. "Few stumble along the well-trodden path," he said to them, adding that he would wait for another opportunity.

The general was in fact right about one thing: the rebels in Ketha were indeed brought down by Molor's troops. But a better opportunity to strike never arose.

Molor had always coveted Kilgore, for it would finally give him a foothold in the sea. He had massed troops to invade when Yorif was warlord, and only Chu'paq's ascension stayed his hand. After the Ketha rebellion was quashed, Molor turned his sights to Chu'paq and the sea that bore his name.

While General Chu'paq waited for the right moment, Molor struck quickly, bringing his forces directly from Ketha to Kilgore Island. Molor slew Chu'paq himself, and now the tyrant was at last a sea power as well as a land power.

Hesitation leads to doubt. And doubt weakens iron.

Two Against Five Hundred

The greatest romance of Klingon history might never have happened had Kahless himself not followed his own advice, that to delay a battle is to lose it.

Kahless was in the Great Hall at Qam-Chee when Molor's troops were readying an attack. Kahless had arranged to meet with several allies who had pledged to stand at his side against the tyrant. Two emissaries came that day from warriors who had decided to remain loyal to Molor.

The first emissary was from Gantin the Mighty. He said Gantin would not go back on his word to Molor to aid a filthy rebel. Kahless said he respected a warrior who kept his word—"Honor," Kahless often said, "is the sharpest blade"—and he allowed the emissary to leave unharmed.

The second emissary was the Lady Lukara, carrying a message for Blaq the Indestructible. She informed Kahless that Blaq also refused to join his cause, for he too had sworn an oath to Molor.

So taken was Kahless with the lady's beauty that he asked her to explain Blaq's actions. Had he not, Lukara would have departed as Gantin's emissary had. He questioned her as to Blaq's reasons. Lukara quickly admitted that Blaq did not care much for oaths and words. She chose to tell Kahless that Blaq had given his word because she saw how Kahless responded to Gantin's emissary.

Admiring the lady's perspicacity, Kahless asked for the true reason. Blaq, Lukara said, considered Kahless's cause unwinnable. Blaq did not earn his nickname by flying his banner over lost causes.

Kahless countered that an honorable cause cannot be lost. Better, he said, to die honorably than to live like a coward. Better nakedness and honor than regalia and cowardice. Lukara said no one had called Blaq a coward and lived. Kahless smiled and said, "Before today, perhaps."

It was then that five hundred of Molor's troops came over the Ni'Dan ridge. The city garrison had pledged their loyalty to Kahless. That was why the meeting was held at Qam-Chee. But at the sight of Molor's forces, the garrison retreated to the other side of the Qam-Chee River, to the Valley of the Wild. Disgusted that the warriors of Qam-Chee preferred to wallow with wild *targ* and *klongat*, Kahless turned to face the oncoming troops without hesitation.

Lukara smiled and unsheathed her own weapon, a great *tik'leth*.

Together, Kahless and Lukara fought Molor's troops, driving them away from the city.

That day, the greatest romance in the history of Qo'noS began.

Later, Lukara would explain that Kahless's words had touched her heart. She took up arms with him knowing that it would give Kahless what he wanted. If they won, she would have proof that Kahless's cause was just and honorable, for how else could he survive such an onslaught? If they lost, they would find her body alongside his wearing Blaq's colors. Molor would believe the Indestructible One had, at the end, pledged his forces against him. Blaq would be forced to take up arms against Molor, granting Kahless his desire to unite all against Molor.

Because Kahless joined the battle immediately, both in speaking with Lukara and in facing Molor's warriors, he won a great battle. Because he acted quickly, he met the woman who would become his mate. Because he saw the thing through to its end, he was victorious many times over.

And, in fact, Blaq the Indestructible joined Kahless's side after Qam-Chee. It was he who mated the two of them on the summit of Soyqi in the Hamar Mountains. The candles used in the ceremony were made from the fat of *targ* native to those mountains, the very animals sacrificed to Blaq in Kahless's and Lukara's names.

The battle you attempt to put off today will ruin you tomorrow.

K'Ratak's commentary

There are those who believe this is a redundant precept. Indeed, in her criticisms of *qeS'a'*, the cleric Lysar used this as an example of the text's inapplicability to modern Klingons. "Perhaps the Klingons of old needed lessons to be repeated to them as if they were small children," she said, "and, therefore, the author thought it necessary to say to 'Strike quickly' in the second precept and then 'Leave nothing until tomorrow' in the seventh."

However, Lysar misses the point of this precept. While the second precept speaks to action, this seventh precept speaks to *inaction*, a subtle but important difference. The second precept assumes that one has already decided to strike, and it emphasizes that doing so quickly is the best path to honorable victory. This precept, on the other hand, concerns the warrior who does not strike at all, whose thoughts have not yet achieved their focus. The seventh teaches why action should be taken in the first place.

A good example of the injunction against inaction is that of the House of Koghima, a minor family. One day, Koghima was at the tavern at B'Alda'ar Base, traveling with his *ghIntaq*, Kazho. Koghima was drinking heavily, and got into an argument with another Klingon. The argument grew heated, as arguments in taverns tend to—nothing extends a fighter's reach like a drained mug—and finally Koghima grew frustrated and walked away. The other Klingon, however, was still angry. He unsheathed his *d'k tahg* and plunged it into Koghima's back.

In that moment, Kazho could have acted. The killer was without honor, for who attacks in shadow believes the cause unjust. Whose cause is unjust forfeits all claim to honor. He stared at the warrior who had so dishonorably killed the man to whom he'd pledged his life. But Kazho did not take action, which allowed the killer to run away. Kazho leapt to Koghima's side, performing the death scream for him.

And then, rather than pursue the killer, he travelled back to the homeworld in order to inform Koghima's mate, Gosek, what had happened. Gosek was furious. Koghima and she had not yet had children, and there was no heir to the House. Gosek's heart cried out for vengeance, and she told Kazho that they needed to find the filthy *petaQ* who took her mate's life in so cowardly a manner.

Kazho thought this action to be foolish, but he was not thinking clearly. He was in love with Gosek, and saw this as an opportunity at last to take what he wanted and become Gosek's mate. But she refused, because Koghima—the head of the House, to whom both she and Kazho were sworn—had not been avenged. Gosek could do nothing until her husband's killer was found.

For many turns, they traveled the Empire in search of Koghima's killer. It was a fool's errand, of course—the Empire is quite large, and Kazho had only a vague, bloodwine-soaked recollection of what the coward looked like. But Gosek's honor demanded that she fulfill her right of vengeance against her mate's killer. There was no greater cause for her, and she would continue to pursue it until the resources of House Koghima were drained, or until she died.

Bound both by his oath to the House and by his love for Gosek—not to mention his knowledge, however hazy, of the killer's face—Kazho searched alongside Gosek. But they never found the coward. Had Kazho done his duty as *ghIntaq*, had he struck when the opportunity presented itself, Gosek's honor would have been fulfilled and Kazho might well have succeeded in becoming her mate. Instead, he was condemned to an endless quest with a woman he loved but who hated him. He did not become the head of a House, nor did he have Gosek's devotion.

Sometimes inaction seems necessary, but a warrior must look deeper. Most agree that the finest bloodwine comes from vintners who toil on the worlds in the Pheben system. But when the planet Zakorg was conquered by the Empire, several farmable tracts of land were discovered there. However, the noblest Houses had first rights to acquire that land. It would be many turns before all of them would have their opportunities to inspect the land and make their decisions.

There were other tracts that were not immediately arable, and so were being sold far more cheaply and to anyone who wished to buy, regardless of class. A former enlisted soldier in the Defense Force and a warrior with no House, Pelgren took the wages he earned as a warrior and purchased the cheaper land on Zakorg.

Experienced vintners laughed at him and mocked him. Even the arable land on Zakorg would take decades to produce good bloodwine. But Pelgren grabbed the opportunity that presented itself, and he worked the land hard, refusing to wait for a chance to purchase finer land and researching how to alter the soil to make it more suitable. The work was backbreaking, but no victory was ever won without toil.

His land became ready to produce wine as quickly as those of the others who had bought seemingly better land on Zakorg at the same time. Today,

Pelgren produces some of the finest bloodwine in the Empire. Pelgren enriched the land with his blood and sweat. The result has benefitted the entire Empire— at least those who appreciate good bloodwine. The others not of noble birth were willing to wait until tomorrow, while Pelgren acted today. The Empire is a better place for his insistence on taking action.

The story of Kahless and Lukara at Qam-Chee is one of our greatest, though documents found by an archeological survey conducted by the Federation on Krios revealed something that many scholars had long believed: Kahless and Lukara did *not* fight off Molor's forces by themselves. So wise is Kahless that all stories about him are instructive, even those that are embellished or altered in the retelling. The historical truth, however, illustrates this precept every bit as well as the philosophical truth of the legend.

The city garrison was led by a warrior named Keeba, who saw Molor's forces coming over the Ni'Dan ridge and thought it would be wise to retreat and regroup at the Valley of the Wild. The story as it was told over the centuries was that Keeba's forces retreated, yes, but the warrior's intent was to let Molor's forces take Qam-Chee and then, under cover of darkness, cross the river again and attack in surprise.

Kahless thought this a poor strategy. He and Lukara argued with Keeba that they needed to face Molor directly, to show themselves as befitted the stature of their opponent. Besides, they maintained, to let Molor take Qam-Chee granted him a victory without a fight. It gave Molor's forces a city to entrench in, which would make the second part of Keeba's plan all the harder to execute. A complicated strategy is like running uphill. Kahless believed the only way to stop Molor's armies was to keep them from crossing the Ni'Dan ridge. Keeba disagreed and ordered his warriors to regroup at the Valley of the Wild, but not all his warriors followed the order. They believed in Kahless and so they stayed to fight by his side—as did Lukara.

But in the end, very few of those warriors survived. Victory belonged to Kahless, but it came at the cost of dozens of lives. Kahless and Lukara both survived, of course, and they owed it all to those members of Keeba's garrison who saw the wisdom in this precept.

It must be marked that the warriors who aided Kahless and Lukara followed their instincts—a worthy impetus—but at the expense of their oaths as soldiers. In so doing, they incurred dishonor. For while a soldier's first allegiance is to honor, and the second to Empire, the third is to commander. It is not a warrior's portion to choose which orders to obey, which tactics to support. Of course, Keeba's order was also tainted. To abandon the city, to attack it in darkness, to practice the subtle art of camouflage, as his scheme entailed—these are not the tactics of a warrior overly concerned with honor. Were the soldiers right to disobey? Would their allegiance to Keeba have been dishonorable?

It is difficult to say. But however they arrived at the field of battle, they fought and died alongside the greatest warrior who ever lived. Whether their actions were foolish, their lives were more than honorable at their ending, and they no doubt rode the River of Blood to *Sto-Vo-Kor*.

Keeba also realized his mistake, and he committed *Mauk-to'Vor*. The records found on Krios were those of his descendants. The documents included a scroll containing Keeba's own final words, written on the day he took his own life with the aid of his lieutenant. What he wrote is worth reprinting here, for it shows insight into not only the way Kahless's contemporaries viewed him, but also this precept.

"My interest in Kahless was always less in who he was than in who was his enemy. I cared little for his philosophy or for his cause. All I knew was I had spent most of my adult life fighting against Molor, and Kahless was a fellow rebel against the tyrant, one who had more success than anyone else in striking worthwhile blows against Molor.

"But I never paid much attention to Kahless himself. My alliance with him was one of convenience. The enemy of my enemy is my comrade, and so I allowed him to meet with emissaries of other warlords he hoped would join us in our battle against Molor.

"When Molor's forces were sighted coming toward the Ni'Dan ridge, I believed that we had a poorer chance of defeating him through normal means. I suggested retreating, regrouping, and surprising Molor once he took the city and became complacent. I wished to put off the conflict until I could find an opportunity to attack that would have a better chance of victory.

"So arrogant was I in believing my strategy to be sound that I refused to heed Kahless when he suggested meeting Molor's forces at the ridge. Who was this rebel to tell me what to do?

"I heard his words, but I did not listen. My own troops, though, had listened, not just to Kahless's strategy for facing Molor, but to his words regarding honor and the other principles he championed. I had allied myself with Kahless, it is true, but many of my troops *believed* in him. I did not. At least not yet.

"Later, after I made my foolish retreat, Kahless stayed behind to fight off Molor's forces, alongside Blaq the Indestructible's emissary and many of my own troops who disobeyed me.

"And they were right to! Kahless won, and all across the land, people are talking of his great victory at Qam-Chee. I took the cautious route and was denied a part in that victory. I have shamed myself, and I have shamed a great man whose greatness I was too arrogant and closed-minded to appreciate."

Keeba realized too late the truth of this precept: inaction breeds complacency, and complacency breeds dishonorable defeat. It is only through action that one can hope to stake a claim to an honorable victory.

Eighth Precept

Choose death over chains.

"A prisoner can only be a victim or a traitor—never a hero."

—Kahless

Victory is triumph, and death is honorable. But the warrior who is captured is denied these prizes and achieves neither glory nor honor. Capture brings only deathless defeat.

DICTUM: THE BROKEN CAGE

WARRIORS MUST HATE ABOVE ALL THE CAGES THAT CONSTRAIN THEM.

IMPRISONED, A WARRIOR FINDS EVERYTHING PRECIOUS TAKEN FROM HIM,

HIS WILL THWARTED. AND WITHOUT THE POWER TO DO ONE'S WILL,

ONE CANNOT BE FREE. CAPTIVITY IS A SHAMEFUL STATE THAT MUST BE

RESISTED, FOR IMPRISONMENT IS A TWILIGHT EXISTENCE WHEREIN ALL

NEEDS GO UNMET, ALL DESIRES UNFULFILLED. THE CAPTIVE LIVES AT

ANOTHER'S PLEASURE AND NEVER HIS OWN. A PRISONER DOES NOT HOLD

THE DEED TO HIS OWN LIFE. THOUGH SOME CAGES ARE CONSTRUCTED BY

CIRCUMSTANCE AND NOT BY MASONS AND SMITHS, AND THOUGH THEY

EXIST ONLY WITHIN THE MIND, THESE TOO MUST BE BROKEN. ANYTHING

THAT WOULD CONFINE YOUR WILL MUST NOT REMAIN.

THE WARRIOR'S CALLING

A warrior, by definition, is someone who makes war. It is not possible to engage in battle when one is restrained.

When warriors battle, they bring honor to themselves, to their families, to their commanders, to their Empire. In victory, they achieve glory. In death, they achieve greatness.

A warrior who fights and wins stands over a defeated foe as proof that glory has been achieved, that virtue has been upheld, that warfare is still the highest art. That honor still matters.

A warrior who fights and loses can take solace in an honorable death and expect to sail across the River of Blood to *Sto-Vo-Kor*.

But a warrior who neither wins nor loses, who fails even to fight? What of this warrior, who earns no honor and acquires no legacy? That warrior's name is banished to the vast halls of the obscure, the unremembered ranks of the failed, the crew of dishonored sailors on the Barge of the Dead.

Victory is triumph, and death is honorable. But the warrior who is captured is denied these prizes and achieves neither glory nor honor. Capture brings only deathless defeat. Your end comes not in glorious combat, but in ignominy.

GENDHET AND THE CAPTIVES

Following Kahless's defeat of Molor, many soldiers loyal to the tyrant fled. Molor's military leader, Warlord Gendhet, gathered those soldiers to fight against Kahless in Molor's name.

Kahless sent General Tygrak, fresh from his victory at Goqlath Mountain, to battle Gendhet. Tygrak believed Gendhet to have only a few hundred warriors at his command. But Molor had not become a tyrant by accident. Many swore loyalty to him, and they did not change their allegiance after Kahless slew their leader.

Tygrak was overwhelmed by superior numbers. Worse, he saw that Gendhet's soldiers had obviously been instructed to maim but not kill—and to take prisoners.

When Tygrak saw this, he was incensed. Bad enough that he was badly overmatched. That was merely a circumstance of warfare. Advantages come and go. Tactics succeed and fail.

But Tygrak would not allow his people to be made Gendhet's prisoners. The warlord had a well-deserved reputation as an interrogator. Tygrak feared that his warriors would become living corpses, soldiers prevented from performing the simplest of duties, objects of no honor. In addition, if they succumbed to Gendhet's techniques, as some surely would, they might reveal valuable intelligence about Kahless's forces and strategies.

Rather than face that possibility, Tygrak commanded his warriors to fight to the death no matter what. The soldiers who were injured continued to fight even as their blood poured onto the battlefield.

Gendhet ordered Tygrak taken alive at all costs. He sent Kela, his finest warrior, after Tygrak. Kela slashed Tygrak's sword arm, destroying his shoulder. Even as Tygrak stumbled on the ground, even as his blood spilled out, he continued to fight. To surrender would lead to his capture, and his capture would lead to dishonor. That he could not allow.

He fought on with his other arm, until Kela severed that arm at the elbow. Undeterred, Tygrak fought still, kicking his opponent, even using his very bulk as a bludgeon.

Only dead warriors have no weapons. He lived and so he fought, unwilling to have his enemy dictate the terms of his fighting.

Kela was forced to kill Tygrak. It was the only way to stop him. Tygrak's warriors fought likewise, and Gendhet gained no prisoners that day.

Gendhet thought Kahless's forces weak, based on how few were sent against him. He therefore sent all his soldiers against Kahless. They were routed at T'Ong Pass. Had Tygrak or any of his warriors been captured, they might well have revealed the true strength of Kahless's forces, whether in the throes of torture or unwittingly in their exhaustion. By choosing honorable death over dishonorable capture, Tygrak lost a battle but aided in winning the war.

No one ever won a victory from a dungeon.

Not all prisons are physical. Circumstances can create intangible prisons every bit as stout as those made of stone and metal. Intangible prisons we must escape from or die.

LUKARA AND QUMWI

When the Lady Lukara battled alongside Kahless against Molor's forces at Qam-Chee, she was mated to QumwI. Both were of noble families in the service of Blaq the Indestructible, and their union helped strengthen Blaq's court. Lukara had no love for QumwI. She accepted the role of emissary to Kahless as much to get away from her mate as anything.

Her love for Kahless was timeless. Her mating with QumwI was a prison of its own kind.

When she returned to Blaq after Qam-Chee, word of her and Kahless's mighty battle had already reached the Indestructible One. Upon seeing Blaq, Lukara explained to him that she would not be a prisoner of her mating with QumwI. Blaq would grant her a divorce and allow her to be with Kahless or he would grant her *Mauk-to' Vor*.

Blaq saw what they accomplished together. He saw the love that Kahless had for Lukara and she for him. And so he spoke to QumwI, who did not hesitate. "These are two who fought off hundreds of Molor's troops. Their victory speaks of the truth of their hearts. I am not so much a fool that I will stand in their way." In recognizing Lukara's and Kahless's honor, QumwI showed his own that day.

Allowing yourself to be captured dishonors everything around you. A warrior must be free or die. To be shackled makes you not a warrior, but simply a fool who chooses mere existence over full, honorable life.

No warrior defeats death. Far better to face it in a manner that brings glory and honor than to shun its domain, earning only shame and regret.

K'RATAK'S COMMENTARY

Klingons must not allow themselves to be taken prisoner. It's difficult to imagine now, but when *qeS'a'* was written, that philosophy hadn't yet become ingrained into our society. Now, of course, it is a cornerstone, at least in part due to the story of Tygrak's battle against Gendhet. Tygrak's refusal to be taken prisoner led to Gendhet's defeat, and it was that victory of Kahless's that cemented his position as the leader of the Klingon people. Gendhet was the last of Molor's allies to fall, and it was his defeat that truly marked the end of the tyrant and the beginning of Kahless's leadership of the Klingon people.

I remember a speaking engagement I had in the Federation a few years ago. A young Trill mentioned that both Klingons and Romulans refuse to be taken prisoner and asked what the difference was. It was a question of genuine curiosity, not the base insinuation that Klingons and Romulans are alike. Because this woman was not uttering that timeworn slur, I answered her with this anecdote:

When Klingons made first contact with the Romulans, it was immediately cause for war. This is hardly surprising, as both nations are empires that thrive on conquest. In their first engagement, the Klingon ship and the Romulan ship destroyed each other. There were dozens of skirmishes after that, but the two that matter to the Trill's question, and to this precept, were the battles at Gamma Eridon and Devron.

At the former location, a Romulan warship engaged a Klingon vessel captained by the legendary Commander Mozam. The battle was mighty, the inhabitants of Gamma Eridon watching from the ground as the two vessels engaged in an epic confrontation above their world. Eventually, Mozam gained the upper hand when he disabled the shields of the Romulan ship. But as Mozam moved in to ensnare the Romulan vessel in a tractor beam, the Romulan commander set off his missiles in their tubes without firing them, causing the ship to explode.

The battle in the Devron system was between two armadas. Our people sent a fleet led by Captain Korga to fight a fleet of Romulan Birds of Prey. The Romulan commander was victorious, destroying four of the ships in the Klingon fleet and losing only one ship from his own. Realizing the battle could not be won, Korga ordered his last two ships to ram the Romulan flagship, obliterating all three.

Romulans will fall on their swords because they believe suicide preferable to capture. The end is proper, but their means are wasteful. At Gamma Eridon, the Romulans destroyed themselves. At Devron, the Klingons destroyed their enemies as well as themselves. In both cases, capture was avoided, which is to the good, but far better to avoid capture in a way that damages your enemies as well. When Romulans see that defeat is inevitable, they will remove themselves from the field of battle by means of suicide rather than risk capture. When Klingons see that defeat is inevitable, they *keep fighting* and do not give up until they are dead or victorious (or both). It is as they say: Every true warrior's dying wish is to have struck but once more. It is that striving, that relentless march toward victory, that sets Klingons apart from all others.

Not all Klingon warriors follow this precept. Indeed, if every Klingon followed every precept, there would be no need for this volume. One of the most despicable examples of a warrior turning his back on the principle of the eighth precept was Captain Worik. While conducting a mission to sabotage a Federation relay station with the aim of preventing them from listening in on our communications, Worik's Bird-of-Prey was defeated by a Starfleet vessel. To the shock of his crew, Worik surrendered rather than see his vessel destroyed. The Starfleet captain took him prisoner and interrogated him. In exchange for the freedom of

his ten surviving crew (one had died in the battle), Worik offered the Federation intelligence regarding a planned attack on Ardan IV.

The Federation had only just formed, and its founding was viewed as a black day in the Empire. The Earthers, Vulcans, Andorians, and Tellarites were now united, and one strong enemy is far more dangerous than four weak ones. The High Council was determined to prevent the Federation's expansion into worlds desired by the Empire, and the attack on Ardan IV was to be the opening salvo in an all-out campaign against Starfleet.

But because Worik was a coward who put the lives of his crew over the good of the Empire—as though his crew would have agreed to the lessening of their worth, the reduction of their status from warrior to mere survivor—he gave aid and comfort to the enemy by revealing the details of the attack on Ardan IV. What should have been a victory was instead a defeat at the hands of the three Starfleet vessels hastily diverted to defend that outpost. Tellingly, the three ship captains who led that attack did *not* allow themselves to be captured. One captain's ship was destroyed in combat, and the other two plunged their vessels into the surface of Ardan IV, rendering it uninhabitable forevermore. Worik's crew were all returned to the Empire, but, to a warrior, they committed *Mauk-to'Vor* rather than continue to live with their commanding officer's dishonor, a blot that stained them as well. Worik himself spent the rest of his life in a Federation prison, eventually dying of old age. A fittingly ignoble end for such a dishonorable wretch!

Sometimes a foe will capture enemies and prevent them from dying. At the time that *qeS'a'* was first set down, the energy weapon had not yet been developed. That technology changed the rules of warfare. Aside from the fact that it increased the number of people who *could* do battle—one need not have skill with a blade to fight, only the ability to aim—it also meant that one could incapacitate without killing. This is necessary when battling in the empty sky of space, for the warrior who wields a blade in a breathless vacuum cannot wage war for long.

But the development of weapons for spacefaring vessels led to handheld versions of the same, and once a technology is introduced it cannot be eliminated. The *ramjep* hatchling cannot be put back in its egg. While most warriors prefer the heft and honest majesty of a *bat'leth*, or the swift and elegant strokes of a *mek'leth*, or the simple and direct fierceness of a *d'k tahg*, the Galaxy is not always so sensible. And only a fool brings a *d'k tahg* to a disruptor fight. This change in warfare meant that warriors could be taken prisoner against their will, insensate.

One warrior to whom this happened was a lieutenant named M'Raq. A good soldier, M'Raq served for many years with distinction in the Defense Force. While serving on the *I.K.S. HoH*, M'Raq was captured by a Romulan fleet that attacked a communications relay in deep space near the Beta Lankal system. The Romulans had boarded the relay station, and M'Raq led the party that beamed over to stop them. But the *HoH* was destroyed and M'Raq and his soldiers were repelled. The Romulans used their disruptors on a setting that incapacitated without killing, leading to the capture of M'Raq and several of his warriors.

For many turns, M'Raq was kept a prisoner and interrogated countless times, but "his was a roof of stone." Never did he surrender any intelligence. Eventually he was returned to the Empire for reasons that remain classified, though one assumes it was some manner of prisoner exchange. Even though M'Raq was resolute in captivity and kept the Empire's secrets, he was broken by the experience. He never reenlisted in the Defense Force. Instead he remained at home and waited for death. The memory of his captivity hung about him like a shroud. When death finally came, M'Raq died, as Worik did, in a bed, without the satisfaction accorded to the victorious. His oldest son, Klag—now a general and commander of the Fifth Fleet—refused to speak to him from the day he decided not to rejoin the Defense Force until the day he died. M'Raq's captivity ushered in only sorrow: dishonor, a military career in ruins, a son sundered from his father, an unheralded death. When you consider the effects of prison on a Klingon, remember what Kahless once said: "A cage makes the biggest *targ* small."

There are ways to endure one's imprisonment with honor. Earlier, I referred to Chancellor Martok and his imprisonment by the Dominion, when he and Worf had their moment of *tova'dok*. The only way prisoners of the Dominion would die was fighting the Jem'Hadar in the ring. However, because Martok and Worf and the other prisoners—Cardassians, Romulans, Breen, humans—were not permitted to die, they had to work to escape. And work they did, and they earned their freedom thereby, and Martok went on to rule the Empire.

Some might say Martok's eventual fate shows that prisoners don't necessarily forfeit honor, but Martok also struggled to escape, which is more than M'Raq managed. Martok refused to accept the demands the enemy had made.

While they imprisoned his body, they could not contain his spirit or his mind. He and Worf both clung to that knowledge, which served as their ladder back into the lofty realms of honor.

A prisoner laboring to escape, constantly endeavoring to shake off the chains of captivity, may yet find honor, but it is better still not to become a prisoner in the first place. After all, the primary reason the Dominion kept Martok alive was so that they could use him as a guide for the Changeling they sent to replace him. That imposter was the primary mover behind the sundering of the alliance with the Federation. Every prisoner is a pawn who must resist being moved by the enemy.

Ninth Precept
Die standing up.

"If you fall down eight times, you should get up nine times."

—Kahless

Kor refused to die. Instead of falling to the Romulans, he held the line against them, willing himself to fight. Indeed, Kor lived for many more decades, before dying in battle during the Dominion War.

Dictum: The Unbowed Warrior

Warriors must die as they lived and live as they will die. A good death is the summit of a life lived to the last moment. As the sea churns, as the storm roars, so warriors meet their ends. They do not bargain. They do not plead. They ask for nothing and concede the same. Death cannot unmake the life a warrior has wrought. When they die, for die they must, they tear themselves from life—every strand at once—always mindful of the mandate under which they etched their names into the tablets of their time: stand upright, as a warrior stands.

THE CHURNING SEA

Falling down is a temporary event, of no more moment than a muscle twitch. When a warrior falls, the next step should be to rise again immediately. Even when death arrives, a warrior should remain standing. Warriors should die as they live: upright, noble, and welcoming the direst conditions and most brutal challenges.

Death is a poor reason not to stand.

Battle does not end until death ends it. There may be breaks in the battle, but the combat endures until there is a victor.

Until a warrior dies, the battle is not—cannot be—over, because the warrior will simply rise, regain the fury of composure, and take up battle again.

The sea will ever churn. So too for a Klingon in battle.

THE FORTRESS AT QA'VARIN

Kahless never allowed himself to stay fallen. When he finally faced off against Molor, holding his *bat'leth*, the sword of honor that he had forged, it was a grand battle. This was at the fortress at Qa'varin, to which Kahless and Lukara had led their forces.

Molor ruled from that fortress. By this time, it was the only land he still held. The men and women of all the tyrant's other lands had either bent their knees to Kahless or lay dead at his feet, struck down by his growing army of honorable Klingons.

To no one's surprise, Molor refused to concede. Even though he had suffered loss after loss, even though it was obvious to even the meanest intelligence that his reign was over, he did not yield. Tyrant he was, but still he nurtured a guttering flame of honor.

When Kahless broke through the gates and confronted Molor in his throne room, he demanded Molor's surrender.

Sitting on his throne, holding a *tik'leth*, Molor gave Kahless his reply: "Many years ago, I entered this room as you did. A weak fool ruled from this very throne. My troops had overcome every force arrayed against us.

"The fool on the throne saw that I had defeated him, and bent his knee to me, giving up his throne. I cast him into the dungeons below this fortress, where he remained until he died. Until his death, any who considered opposing me were brought to those dungeons and shown the face of the last person to take up arms against me.

"But I will not surrender to you, Kahless. You have poisoned our world with your fancy tales of honor and glory. You have transformed Klingons into weaklings who value concepts and words over might and strength. I do not wish to endure such a place. So I will not bend my knee to you as that fool did before me. Instead, I will fight you and one of us will die. And either way, I will be spared having to live in a world ruled by your idiocy."

Kahless smiled, then. "You say you reject my teachings, yet you face me as a warrior. You revel in glory and fight to the death rather than surrender to a foe who has declared himself your enemy. You already live in a world changed, Molor."

Molor stood and raised his *tik'leth*. "Enough! The time for words is passed! Face me with that foolish weapon of yours and let us end this!"

THE TWO VICTORIES

Before Kortar slew the gods, he fought against the giant *ngeng roQ*,[38] a creature ten times his size, doing battle with it for an entire day.

One of the gods Kortar slew was Khoss the Gigantic, a mighty god who had fought his cousin Migmek the Trickster for seven days and seven nights over a joke Migmek had played.

Kahless himself fought his brother for twelve days because of a lie.

But these fabled battles were as nothing compared to the contest between Molor and Kahless. All through the fortress, the battle raged, Molor's *tik'leth* striking against Kahless's *bat'leth*. They thrust, they parried, they retreated, they attacked.

For days, their combat rang out. For days, Lukara and the forces of Kahless watched, alongside what was left of Molor's forces. For days, they waited for a victor.

In the end, both warriors' bodies were ravaged. Both had bled upon the fortress of Qa'yarin, tyrant's blood mixing with that of the greatest warrior.

Barely able to stand, barely able to raise their weapons, they fought on. Neither would surrender. Each insisted on fighting until he could fight no longer.

Molor lunged with his blade, cutting into Kahless's belly. Kahless stumbled backward, but did not fall. The sword slipped from Molor's grip, still

---

38   The *ngeng roQ* is now extinct, though bones have been found in the bottom of the oceans of Qo'noS. It was amphibious, and a full *kellicam* long. In fact, some believe the measurement was derived from the size of the *ngeng roQ*.

embedded as it was in Kahless's body. Kahless whirled the sword of honor over his head and slashed Molor's neck with the leading blade.

The warriors still stood. But even as the blood poured from Kahless's belly and Molor's neck in torrents, only one warrior was armed. Kahless swung his *bat'leth* and severed Molor's head from his body.

Kahless won two victories that day, one against an opponent, one for an Empire. Molor lived as a tyrant who cared nothing for honor. He died a Klingon who battled to the end, and in so doing, he claimed a scrap of honor, in spite of himself.

It is not enough to fight. A true warrior continues to fight until fighting is no longer possible. And fighting becomes impossible only upon death.

K'RATAK'S COMMENTARY

Kor was one of the great *Dahar* Masters of history. His battles were many—against the Federation at Organia, at Caleb IV, and in the Delta Triangle; against the Romulans at Klach D'Kel Bracht, at Romii, and in the Ionite Nebula; against the Kinshaya at Ikalia, at T'Gha, and in the Q'Tahl cluster; against T'nag at the Korma Pass; against Qagh the Albino at Secarus IV; and, in his final battle, against the Jem'Hadar in the Kalandra Sector. But one battle in particular, the one that earned Kor the title of *Dahar* Master, perfectly illustrates this precept.

A Romulan invasion force hid in Fek'lhr's Belt and ambushed Kor's fleet. Within minutes, all the other ships in the fleet were destroyed, and Kor's flagship, the *Klothos*, was badly damaged. Kor managed to destroy one Romulan ship, but in the battle the *Klothos* lost its shields. A Romulan boarding party beamed aboard the *Klothos* and killed most of Kor's crew.

Kor was near defeat; some might say he *was* defeated. But he absolutely refused to fall. Instead he sent out a distress call and then, armed only with a disruptor and a *bat'leth*, he kept the invaders at bay. The *Klothos* had been his ship for many turns, and he was able to move freely through the access tubes and the dark corners of the vessel, coming out only to confront individual members of the boarding party, picking them off one by one. Several of the Romulans were able to wound Kor before the *Dahar* Master killed them, but still Kor did not fall.

Eventually, the entire boarding party was slaughtered. By the time the Romulan fleet commander realized he had not defeated Kor, the Klingon reinforcements had arrived. The Seventh Fleet made short work of the Romulans.

Kor refused to die. Instead of falling to the Romulans, leading to an invasion of our space, he held the line against them, willing himself to fight. Indeed, Kor lived for many more decades, serving in both the Defense Force and the Diplomatic Service before dying in battle during the Dominion War, the only fitting end for a warrior whose identity was braided with his love and respect for glorious battle.

All those who train as officers in the Defense Force must pass an initiation that puts their understanding of this precept to the test. The trainees are taken to the prison planet Rura Penthe, a harsh and frozen world suitable only for criminals who do not deserve the honor of dying. Each warrior is dropped into the middle of a wide expanse of ice without food or weapons and is told to walk to the Defense Force outpost at the north pole. The trainees are told neither how far they must go, nor which direction north is. They know nothing of the obstacles in their path.

If the trainees survive attacks by wild animals and if they aren't crushed by an avalanche and if they don't succumb to the cold (and, of course, if they determine which direction north is), then they are more likely to pass the test. If they reach the area near the pole, they come across a thin patch of ice that cannot possibly support a Klingon's weight. Most end their test there, for the patch is at least six hours away from the beam-down point, and so by the time any warriors make it there, they cannot survive plummeting into the frigid water underneath the ice. At that point, they're beamed out and allowed to heal. They have passed the test.

Few warriors have ever made it past the thin ice, and those who have were able to construct rafts from some of the thicker shards of ice. Using icicle shards both to row the raft and to clear a path through the water, they were able to sail through the water before it could freeze over. It is worth noting that every single one of the warriors who made it past the ice would later ascend at least to the rank of commander.[39] Those warriors still live and serve or have died honorably in battle.

It is not only warriors who know to die on their feet.

---

39   Generally, Klingon officer ranks are translated into their equivalent Starfleet ranks. Those who survive and succeed in officer training begin at a rank generally translated as "ensign," followed by "lieutenant," "commander," and "captain." Shipmasters are given one of the latter two ranks, "commander" for smaller vessels, "captain" for larger ones. The one exception to the Starfleet-analogue rule is that "general" is used for the equivalent of a Starfleet admiral. Enlisted soldiers are given the rank of *bekk*, along with opportunities to be promoted to the ranks of "leader" and beyond that to *QaS DevwI'*, which literally means "the one who guides the troops," the equivalent of an Army sergeant.

One of the most important farming worlds in the Empire is Pheben III. One of the most successful farms on the planet was owned by a woman named K'Zin. One year, a tornado arose nearby. Undaunted, K'Zin activated the force field that would protect her crops from the storm.

But then the generator failed. K'Zin immediately ran out of the house to tend to it. She did not allow the violent winds to carry her away as she repaired the generator, battered by the elements all the while. She stood her ground long enough to fix the generator, activating the force field, and saving the crops. Only moments after the equipment was functional, the enormous funnel plucked K'Zin from the ground, carried her off, and battered her against a rocky ridge. Had she not acted as she did, she would have lived, yes. But in that case, her family would have had nothing, neither for themselves nor for market, and they would have starved. K'Zin's death was as proud as any warrior's, and she accrued as much honor as any soldier who falls in noble combat. That humble farmer understood that Klingons never let their enemies dictate the terms of battle.

Warriors know that while their hearts beat, battles do not end. And though warriors may stumble, an honorable warrior truly falls only once.

Tenth Precept

Guard honor
above all.

"Honor is what separates Klingons from the beasts of the field."

—Kahless

Kahless tracked Morath down to the shores of the Bazho River. For twelve days and twelve nights, brother fought against brother in desperate combat. They used no weapons, fighting only with fist and foot.

DICTUM: THE HIGHEST PEAK

WARRIORS MUST CLIMB. WHEN THEY CREST THE MOUNTAIN OF HONOR, ALL IS PLAIN: THE PITFALLS AND PERILS, THE SHEER FACES AND DEAD DROPS. EVERY POSSIBILITY OF SUCCESS AND FAILURE. THE WAY IS CLEAR. THOUGH IT WINDS AND DOUBLES BACK, THOSE AT THE TOP CAN SEE IT AS THOUGH IT WERE LIT WITH FLAME. THIS IS THE ADVANTAGE HONOR BESTOWS: A CLARITY OF VISION, A BEARING UNSHAKABLE AS THE ROOTS OF MOUNTAINS. THE HONORABLE SEE. THEY UNDERSTAND. ALL IS BEFORE THEM, SPREAD OUT LIKE THE TUMBLED LAND BELOW TOWERING PEAKS. SCALING THE CLIFFS DEMANDS STRENGTH, WILL, AND COURAGE, AND IT EXACTS A TOLL OF SWEAT AND BLOOD AND PAIN. BUT STANDING AT THE UTMOST HEIGHT OF HONOR, A WARRIOR HAS CONQUERED DEMONS.

WARRIORS AND TRUTH

There are many components to honorable behavior, but the foremost of these is truth. All aspects of honor derive from honesty. A liar cannot truly be honorable, for where is the honor in deception?

Battle reveals a warrior's true self, and in many ways, lies are not possible in battle. When warriors fight, they reveal their inner selves. The purity of warfare allows nothing else. A true warrior knows that the battle does not end until death, and so combat is a lifelong pursuit.

If combat is the only lasting condition, then the warrior's true face must be the same. There is no place in combat for deception. A true warrior accepts no deception in any aspect of life. Deception is a heavy stone.

Children lie all the time, for they are young and do not know better. Kahless spoke often of his own youth, of growing up with his brother Morath. When they were young, they would play at fighting each other in the manner of children. Once, in their fighting, they broke a valuable sculpture that had been in their family for longer than anyone could remember.

Morath and Kahless both agreed to tell their parents that their pet *targ* was responsible. Their parents believed the story, for the *targ* was wild and often had the run of the house. Callow youths that they were, they were proud of their deception, and relieved at having avoided their parents' wrath.

Later, when he matured, Kahless realized he had made the wrong choice. But children are expected to make bad choices. If they do not, they do not learn to become adults. Who doesn't fail will not learn.

Kahless once said that children's mistakes are perfect, for they serve an honorable purpose. Children's false steps eventually take them away from the path of illusion and selfishness and onto the road of honor.

Only those who understand their failures for what they are can learn from them, however. Making the same mistake more than once shows a paucity of reason.

THE TWELVE DAYS' BATTLE

When they were adults, Morath, not having learned the lessons of youth, told a lie and took credit for a battle he did not win. In fact, he lost the battle and retreated rather than stay to finish the fight and die honorably.

Kahless was disgusted, and he condemned his brother for dishonoring his cause, their family, and the very notion of proper combat. Seeing how angry his brother was, Morath fled from his wrath.

Giving chase, Kahless eventually tracked Morath down to the shores of the Bazho River. For twelve days and twelve nights, brother fought against brother in desperate combat. They used no weapons, fighting only with fist and foot. Every time Kahless caught up to his brother or got the better of him, Morath retreated, compounding his dishonor a hundredfold.

It was not merely that Morath lied, but that he refused to admit he had lied, and then ran when confronted with it. He added links to the chain of his lie and bound himself with it. His one lie started a sequence of events that led to a twelve-day battle with his own brother, and it could have been avoided by simply telling the truth.

Nothing is simpler than the truth. For an honorable Klingon, speaking it is an impulse impossible to resist.

On Reason and Honor

When Kahless said that honor was what separated Klingons from the beasts of the field, a young man named Kropar replied, "That is ridiculous. What separates us from the beasts of the field is that we are capable of reason."

Kahless regarded the youth with amusement. "Does not the *ramjep* bird avoid the talons of the *trigak* by flying high above the tree line, where it cannot be caught? That is the act of a rational creature."

Kropar was not deterred. "We are tool users."

"That is mere biology," Kahless countered. "The position and use of our thumbs is not what makes us Klingon. What makes us Klingon is that we're *aware* of concepts such as honor. A *klongat* has no conception of honor. It knows only that it must survive. Everything a beast does, from the rankest *chuSwI'* to the grandest *khrun*, is solely in the service of survival.

"But we are *Klingons*. We are more than simply beings who eat to survive so we can eat another day. We understand and extol the importance of truth, honor, and courage. And that is why it is imperative that we build our lives upon those concepts. Unless we do, we are no different from beasts."

Without truth, there is no honor. Without honor, we are not Klingons, but only tool-wielding animals with no power to shape our world, to conquer space, or to rewrite the history of our time.

K'RATAK'S COMMENTARY

With this precept, the last of them, every strand of Klingon warmaking and honorable behavior is knotted together, as all the precepts lead to this. Choosing your enemies, striking quickly, facing your enemy, seeking adversity, revealing your true self, destroying weakness, leaving nothing until tomorrow, choosing death over chains, and dying standing up all lead to this precept.

Some would argue—indeed, many have—that this is the only precept in *qeS'a'* that matters. If you behave honorably, if you tell the truth, if you put honor before everything else, then all the other precepts will flow naturally from that as blood flows from a Klingon's heart.

Perhaps most importantly, if a Klingon gives his or her word, that word is sacrosanct. When a Klingon has promised something, it will be done. A Klingon's promise is made of duranium: steadfast, irrefutable. A Klingon's promise is fundamental. It is axiomatic.

When storytellers speak of the *Dahar* Master Kang, they always discuss his battles against the Starfleet vessels *Enterprise* and *Excelsior* or his battles alongside fellow *Dahar* Masters Kor and Koloth against T'nag at the Korma Pass or the trio's lengthy campaign against Qagh the Albino, who killed all three of their sons.

But my favorite story about Kang is one that's almost never told. He served as first officer on the *Krim's Run* under Captain L'Kaln. That vessel was assigned to Kromrat, a small colony under regular attack by depredators. Kang beamed down to the surface of Kromrat, and gave his word to the colonists—primarily farmers—that the *Krim's Run* would not bombard from orbit, damaging their farms.

The depredators made their first attempt on Kromrat, and the *Krim's Run* failed to stop them from beaming down to the planet. Angered by this setback, L'Kaln ordered orbital bombardment. Kang insisted that the strategy was ill-advised, that that would destroy the very farms they had come to protect. That did not move L'Kaln, as he considered the farms of little interest to the Empire. He claimed they had other methods of obtaining food, and they did not need weaklings who chose tilling soil over wielding a blade.

The first officer then tried to appeal to his captain's honor: Kang had given his word they would not bombard from orbit. To a true Klingon, that should have been enough. However, L'Kaln's only response was that Kang was a fool to make such a promise, and besides, they were only farmers. A word given to a warrior is inviolable, the captain insisted, but a word given to a farmer? Meaningless.

L'Kaln did not understand the point of honor. Klingons tell the truth to protect their own honor, not that of the people to whom they are speaking. It does not matter if one's word is given to warriors, farmers, opera singers, or *jeghpu'wI'*, or even to enemies. If a Klingon makes a promise, that should be the end of the matter. A Klingon's word locks the door.

Worse, there was no reason to bombard from orbit. Kang saw that L'Kaln simply wished the assignment to end, regardless of who was harmed in the process.

Realizing that L'Kaln did not understand honor, Kang challenged his captain. They fought on the bridge of *Krim's Run*, each armed with a *d'k tahg*. Their battle was fierce, but the outcome was never in doubt, for Kang had honor on his side, and L'Kaln had nothing but cowardice. When L'Kaln lay dead at his feet that day, Kang declared himself captain. This started him on the road that led to his becoming one of the most respected warriors in the Empire. Kang has captained many vessels: the *Doj*, the *SuvwI'*, the *Voh'tahk*, the *Klolode*, the *K'tanco*, the *HaH'vat*, the *Sompek*, and many more. And he led them all with far greater honor and courage than the warrior from whom he rightfully wrested command of *Krim's Run*.

Then there was Captain Kadi of the *Death's Hand*. Kadi was ordered to conquer the planet of Mizaria. But when he arrived, he found a planet of pacifists. The Mizarians did not fight back and offered no resistance to the Klingons, surrendering immediately. Strictly speaking, Kadi's standing orders were to bombard the surface until the Mizarians could be induced to surrender. But instead, they capitulated immediately.

Kadi's first officer insisted that they carry out their orders, but—while Kadi would gladly plant the Klingon flag there—he would not needlessly kill beings who would not fight back.

There is no honor in killing a foe who simply waits to die.

It is truth that leads to honor, honor that leads to victory, and victory that leads to strength. We are Klingons, and we are always strong, and that strength comes from our honor. As long as we continue to follow these precepts, we will continue in our position as the victorious guardians of honor.

When Kahless lived, he knew of no other beings in the universe. The Klingon Empire barely covered the majority of Qo'noS. But now, thanks to Kahless's teachings, ours is one of the mightiest empires in the Galaxy, a force to be reckoned with. We are feared by our enemies and respected by our allies, and we control many worlds.

And it is because we guard honor above all.

AFTERWORD

If you have read through this entire volume before coming to this afterword, it will perhaps surprise you to learn that I did not read *qeS'a'* until I was well into adulthood.

Over the last several decades, I have become an authority on *qeS'a'*. This is not the first edition I have annotated, though it is by far the most extensive, and I have given many a talk on the book. Yet, while most highborn Klingons, and indeed many a lowborn Klingon as well, read the book not long after their Age of Ascension, I did not. My parents thought little of the book, and did not encourage me to read it. Father described the book as a "relic of a bygone age, useful for clerics, perhaps, but not for modern Klingons." And Mother was even more succinct: "If I want the wisdom of Kahless, I'll read the sacred texts, not some anonymous idiot's interpretation of them."

As a good son, I did as my parents bade me. What's more, when queried as to whether or not I had read *qeS'a'*, I parroted their reasoning. After all, if it wasn't good enough for my parents, then it wasn't good enough for me to waste my time with, either!

It was when I was in the midst of working on my first novel, *qul naj*, that I was finally convinced to read *qeS'a'*. I was struggling with a particular scene in which the protagonist, Qovar, has his first confrontation with Morval. One of my childhood friends was K'Nera, who eventually became a ship captain—he was killed in battle against Maquis rebels in the days before the Dominion War—and he recommended that I read *qeS'a'*, specifically the Fifth Precept. "I believe," he said, "that you will find it valuable in finding your way through Qovar and Morval's battle."

I laughed at K'Nera, and again said what my parents always said. "That book was written when the Empire was nascent. We hadn't even ventured into space yet! We hadn't colonized Boreth or Ty'Gokor or any other worlds, we hadn't developed energy weapons, we were still ruled by emperors, and the only other species we even knew of were the Hur'q. What possible use could such blatherings from ancient times be to me writing about a modern Klingon?"

K'Nera regarded me with derision. "Have you never even read the text?"

"Of course not," I told him. I scoffed when I did so. "As I said, it is of no use to a modern Klingon."

"Are the words of Kahless of no use to a modern Klingon?"

I did not succumb to this bit of rhetorical trickery. "That is different. Kahless was divine."

"Perhaps. But there is wisdom to be found in old things. After all, do we not still fight with the *bat'leth* even though we have disruptor pistols? Do we not hunt though we have replicators?"

Eventually, I gave in to my friend, partly out of respect for his judgment, and partly because it would end the argument, which had grown tedious. Or, at least, that was what I told myself and him. In truth, I wished the argument to end because he was winning it. I was young and callow, and so I let him win the argument without ever admitting it to him.

I acquired a copy of the book—it was an edition published shortly after K'mpec ascended to the chancellorship—and after I had my evening meal, I sat down with a padd and read the Fifth Precept, intending only to read that and then go to sleep.

Instead, I stayed up the entire night. After reading the Fifth Precept, I went back and read all of it, from First through Tenth, including a re-read of the Fifth, and then I read it again.

I was, to say the least, captivated.

There is a saying among humans that there is no fanatic greater than a convert, and that was certainly the case with me. I went from disdaining a book that I had never read to becoming a fierce advocate, believing it should be read by all Klingons. I started arguing with my friends and family and colleagues about it. (K'Nera looked on in amusement at most of these discussions.) Many hadn't read it since their Age of Ascension—many warriors include the reading of it as part of the preparation for the ceremony or the first task to be done afterward—and they found new wisdom in the words that they could not appreciate in their youth.

I even got my parents to read it, and my father grudgingly admitted that the book had its good points. My mother did not—she threw the padd across the room after finishing the First Precept, deriding the text as "utter nonsense."

To that point, I had written about a third of *qul naj*, and it had taken me several months to get that far. But after devouring *qeS'a'* in a single night, I found myself inspired and filled with even greater purpose. The remaining two-thirds of the novel was finished in two months. K'Nera was correct in the applicability of the Fifth Precept to the first confrontation between Qovar and Morval: Morval showed his true face, and Qovar would do likewise in their

climactic battle atop Kang's Summit. But the influence of *qeS'a'* can likely be seen throughout the manuscript.

After I had finished *qul naj*, and after it had become a success, I toured the Empire, holding gatherings to discuss the novel with Klingons from all over. In every talk, the subject of *qeS'a'* came up, and I enjoyed discussing it with people of all sorts. As a highborn Klingon, I grew up primarily around Defense Force personnel and politicians. Touring for *qul naj* allowed me to meet Klingons from many walks of life, many of whom were not only not warriors, but they had no interest in becoming warriors or even the ability to do so.

However, most of them had read *qeS'a'*. I was stunned, as I had thought it to be a guide for warriors, not farmers or menial workers or teachers or construction workers or the like. Yet they all found wisdom in the words of *qeS'a'*.

One teacher said it changed his life, and that he did not allow the students in his care to move forward in their studies until they could explain the meaning of all ten precepts to him in detail.

A farmer told me how she made all her children and grandchildren read it, and they would sing the song every *yobta yupma'* with her family. (She was also the one who told me the story of K'Zin that I used in my commentary on the Ninth Precept.)

Even a janitor was able to find wisdom in the precepts. This old man who had a barely functioning left leg and the responsibility for supervising the cleaning of the floors in the Lukara Edifice, and who could claim membership in no House, told me that he read *qeS'a'* every day before he began work, and applied the precepts to his work. Even though the only foe he ever truly faces is the dirt tracked by boots on the edifice floors, it is still one he must defeat every day.

It was with a renewed sense of purpose that I re-read the book after the tour, again finding new truths in it. Meeting other Klingons not of the warrior caste helped me understand all over again what a great book this is.

I found myself reminded of the truth of honor, that it is not something set in stone and on parchment, but rather in blood and bone, and what family a Klingon is born to matters less than the fact that we *are* Klingons. We live for honor, and without honor we are nothing. And our honor comes from within, not without.

But when the book was released to other nations, I found myself expanding the tour beyond our borders. It was my first time ever leaving the Empire, and I found myself apprehensive. But the Fourth and Sixth Precepts rang in my mind. My reluctance to exit the Empire was adversity that I needed to seek and simultaneously weakness I needed to destroy.

One of the first engagements I had was in the Federation, at a university on Berengaria. The first question I was asked was what the biggest influence was on my writing, and the only answer I could give was *qeS'a'*. At that point, very few copies of this text had made it outside the Empire—though the professor who hosted the event had read it—and so I had to explain the work.

That became the theme of the tour. While I spoke at great length about *qul naj* and its themes and metaphors, I also talked at equal length about *qeS'a'* and its importance to Klingon life in general and to my writing in particular.

I later made a similar tour outside the Empire when *yoj nIyma'* was released, but by that time, *qeS'a'*—inspired, or so I was told, by demand created by my own talking up of the book—had been made available in translation throughout the Federation, as well as many non-aligned worlds. I even heard rumors that unauthorized editions were published in the Ferengi Alliance, though I shudder to think how they translated the precepts. In fact, I recall reading a lengthy treatise by a Federation scholar named Sonek Pran, comparing *qeS'a'* to the Rules of Acquisition, and the influence that the two texts had on our respective cultures.

That second tour was especially enlightening, because I heard from so many different cultures—the Federation has not one culture, but a multitude, a concatenation that should be a chaotic disaster, yet somehow they make it work—on the subject of what *qeS'a'* meant to them.

There was the human traffic controller. "My life is simple, but also meaningless. We've eliminated want and need to such a degree that sometimes I wonder if there's anything worth fighting for. Indeed, anything worth doing. When I read *The Klingon Art of War*"— this is how the title is translated in the Federation for some reason, though I question whether *art* is the appropriate word—"I realized that all of life is a fight, and you just have to know where to look for it."

Then there was the Vulcan philosopher. (That is actually an occupation on Vulcan. They are a strange species.) "I found the precepts to be surprisingly logical. While the barbarity of the descriptions of warfare are distasteful, the underlying principles behind them are sound. In particular, I admire the concept of seeking adversity. As Vulcans, we strive for intellectual challenges, and while the pursuit of a point of logic or a scientific inquiry may not be the same as a

glorious battle to be won, the concept of challenging oneself is still a valid one, and a lesson that many could afford to learn."

A Betazoid skimmer pilot came to me after one talk. "As a telepath, I found the notion of revealing your true face to be fascinating. People often assume that we are able to see people's true faces, simply because we have access to their thoughts, but it simply isn't so. The humanoid brain is far too chaotic and nonsensical. The ability to read thoughts may occasionally provide deeper insight into someone, but it does not reveal someone's true face. Only in adversity and trying circumstances do people figure out who they really are, it seems."

And then there was the Cardassian assayer, who was confused when he read the book. "This is an outdated work. I mean, yes, it was useful once, I suppose, when you were barbarians hunting for your food without any interest in the Galaxy beyond your world, but now? You have spaceships and energy weapons, who cares about that nonsense about hunting or fighting people hand to hand?"

There was the Bolian computer analyst, who started studying *mok'bara* because she read about it in *qeS'a'*. There was the Benzite doctor who hated the last precept, but admired the first nine. There was the Pahkwa-thanh musician who particularly loved the Fourth Precept, as his species are also hunters. There was the Andorian ice sculptor who told me that he loved my book, but hated *qeS'a'*—but that he did start playing *klin zha* because of it. And there was the Tellarite ambassador who said the book changed her life so much that she was requesting a diplomatic posting to the Empire. (She didn't get it.)

Most intriguing, however, was the Bynar pair who found the book incomprehensible. A species that is interlinked with their computers, the Bynars simply did not understand the precepts, interpreting them far too literally. For example: "How can you show your true face in combat when it's the same face that you show at all other times? Klingons are not shapeshifters." Even the ones they thought they did comprehend—like **Strike quickly or strike not**—they did not interpret properly. They viewed the Second Precept as a guide to the dual nature of life, reasoning that one can do only a thing or its opposite.

Their biggest complaint, though, was throughout the entire book, they never once encountered a definition of honor.

I must admit that I laughed for a very long time in the face of those Bynars, which was all I could do when confronted by such a ridiculous statement.

Honor is a code that we follow, but to define it like some kind of laboratory experiment or mathematical equation is to simplify it beyond all reason. Indeed, I could publish another entire book twice the size of this edition of *qeS'a'* as a guide to honorable behavior and still come no closer to a dictionary definition that would satisfy those Bynars.

The only way to define honor is that it is how we better ourselves. The universe is a difficult, unpleasant, dangerous place, and the more we discover, the more unpleasant it becomes. Before Kahless, we squabbled amongst ourselves, as Qo'noS was awash in petty fiefdoms before the Unforgettable One brought us all together in the cause of honor. After Kahless, the Hur'q came and introduced us forcibly to a universe that would not treat us well, a universe that forced us to fight back.

As we explored farther into space, we found more enemies: the Romulans, the Kinshaya, the Kreel, the Federation, the Tholians. And then the Bajoran wormhole opened up the Gamma Quadrant, which led to battle against the Dominion. Then the Borg, then the Typhon Pact . . . The Galaxy has not ceased to remind us that there are enemies who will stop at nothing to destroy us.

While we have found allies in the black sky, we have also found that we must set ourselves above those who would take our Empire away from us. As Kahless said before he ascended to *Sto-Vo-Kor*, we are Klingons, and we need no one but ourselves. The way we keep ourselves above all other species is that we live our lives by a code that defines us, that elevates us, that improves us.

It does not matter if we are a single species on a single planet or an empire that spans dozens of solar systems: the precepts of honor remain the same. With all respect to my mother, to the Bynars, to the Cardassian, the greatness of *qeS'a'* is that it is universal. Honor does not change with the passage of time, with the revelation that there are more species in the universe than we once believed. Honor does not wilt before strong foes, it thrives.

Honor is what makes us Klingons.

APPENDIX A
THE WARRIOR'S EDGE: ON THE HISTORY AND USES OF BLADED WEAPONS

Continuing advances in technology have allowed the Empire to grow and flourish. As a consequence, also improved is our ability to wage war upon our rivals, which have only increased in number after we Klingons ventured forth from the confines of our cherished homeworld and traveled to other planets in our ongoing hunt for conquest.

Despite all it has given us, technology also carries the potential to take from us that which we most hold dear: our very identity. Ours is a legacy of conflict, forged from humble beginnings in the heat of battle and cooled by the blood of our enemies. It is a heritage handed down to us by our ancestors throughout our long history. The hard-won lessons of the past endure, offering knowledge and sage counsel to those with the wisdom to observe and revere what has come before. To do so through word and deed is the mark of a true, honorable warrior.

One means of demonstrating this unwavering respect is through our continued devotion to a finely honed blade. Though primitive projectile weapons have long since given way to phased energy and particle beam disruptors, there remains within the foundation of our culture a deep reverence for older, simpler, and more brutal instruments of conflict. Modern armaments serve us well, but demonstrating proficiency in their use really is no more demanding than any another duty required of the soldier. Conversely, mastering the art of edged weapons requires focus and dedication far beyond that needed to obtain expertise in simple marksmanship.

Spears, knives and swords have been with us since before the founding of the Empire itself, reminding us of the struggles we endured as a people before Kahless the Unforgettable set us upon the true path to honor and glory. When employed properly, the blade becomes an extension of its wielder's body, attacking and defending as though animated by its own impulses, as though possessed of its owner's will. Such is combat at its most pure.

As it always has been, Klingons are given opportunity to learn and handle such weapons well before adolescence and the First Right of Ascension. Given the chance, most warriors likely will tell you similar tales of reaching the Age of Inclusion and receiving from their father a *d'k tahg* bearing their family crest. They may describe the *bat'leth* hanging on their home's trophy wall, and perhaps even regale you with a story of the honored relative to whom it once belonged. This is our shared legacy, and it is incumbent upon all of us to see that it remains relevant for those who one day will step forward to serve the Empire in our stead.

Bat'leth

This is perhaps the oldest weapon known to our culture. It certainly is the oldest to be forged by the hands of any Klingon. All Klingons have heard the story of Kahless molding the first *bat'leth* centuries ago, using his creation to defeat the tyrant Molor before founding what we now call the Klingon Empire. Through the ages, this weapon has been refined through the use of ever-improved materials and techniques, but at its heart the *bat'leth* remains unchanged, a symbol as eternal as the Empire itself. Indeed, this weapon is a coveted acquisition among many outworlders, particularly Romulans, Tzenkethi, and even humans.

Mastery of the *bat'leth* comes only after years of dedicated practice. Many warriors spend their entire lives perfecting its use, longing for the day when they can bring it to the fore against a worthy adversary. Unlike other edged weapons, the *bat'leth* has a size, weight and design requiring its wielder to move in harmony with the blade. An awareness of one's body's position relative to the weapon and one's opponent as well as the surroundings is critical if one is to emerge victorious from combat with a *bat'leth*. There are those who believe such proficiency is achieved through a balance of art, grace, and tactical application, each enhanced by other, intangible qualities, such as the warrior's being in tune with the beating his own heart, the air filling his lungs, and the rush of blood through his veins. Klingons who have advanced to the highest levels of aptitude with the *bat'leth* are known to train with their eyes covered, forcing their other senses to become more attuned to their environs.

Those who distinguish themselves in battle can find themselves honored by induction into the Order of the *Bat'leth*, one of the Klingon Empire's highest military awards. This ancient society founded by Lady Lukara, the widow of Kahless, is charged with upholding the principles he set forth for the honor of the Empire. Those who wear the medallion of the Order are understood to be warriors without peer.

D'k tahg

This is often the first edged weapon to which a young Klingon is exposed, just as it is almost always the first they carry as their own. Like the *bat'leth*, this knife embodies a storied history, passed, as it is, generation after generation, from father to son. Proudly displayed on one's belt, the *d'k tahg* symbolizes its owner's status as a warrior of the Empire.

In combat, this knife often supplements its wielder's fighting prowess as well as the strength of his mind, body, and heart. Contests fought with *d'k tahg* are usually of a personal nature, such as when defending against a challenge to one's honor or the standing of one's house. Indeed, given that many *d'k tahg*s are emblazoned with the emblem of one's family, taking this weapon from a warrior—whether through simple theft or as a spoil of victory during battle—is considered a grave insult not only to the individual but also to his clan. For this reason alone, many Klingons treasure these blades and all they represent, and they will gladly die before surrendering them to an enemy.

The *d'k tahg* also plays a prominent role in certain long-standing sacraments, such as paying respect to a fallen warrior by using a blade to extinguish the flame that represents his life. This is meant to be carried out with a weapon of personal value, and the *d'k tahg* exemplifies its owner's character and loyalty as he assists in ensuring his deceased comrade's entry into *Sto-Vo-Kor*.

ghIntaq

Also possessing a long and distinguished history, the *ghIntaq* is not a knife or sword but rather a spear that features a knife blade at one end and a heavy, blunt base. While other spears are used for hunting and even for sporting competition, the *ghIntaq*'s sole purpose is for battle. The weapon is employed in multiple ways, both thrust in hand-to-hand combat and thrown from farther distances. Experienced Klingons often use a *ghIntaq* in tandem with a *mek'leth* when engaging enemies in close quarters.

In ancient times, the Emperor's personal guards carried ceremonial *ghIntaq*s, far heavier and with blades much longer and sharper than their counterparts used by the conventional military. Imperial guards were well trained in the use of the spear as well as the *tik'leth* sword, making them formidable opponents for anyone who might wish to do the

Emperor harm. Today, this level of expertise with the *ghIntaq* is a rarity among all but the oldest and most battle-tested warriors.

qutluch

A holdover from ancient times and rites of passage, as well as when formal public executions were far more prevalent than they are today, the *qutluch* continues to occupy a privileged place in our culture. It is often is used to inflict an adolescent's first bloodletting in preparation for his Rite of Ascension, which begins his path to warriorhood.

Despite being relegated largely to ceremonial use, the *qutluch* is often found in the hands of assassins, Klingon and otherwise. Of course, this taints the weapon's place of distinction within our shared heritage, to the point where some houses have taken to using family *d'k tahgs* or even *mevaks* for initiating the Rite of Ascension.

Mek'leth

Smaller than the *bat'leth*, this weapon requires no less dedication of the warrior's mind and spirit. It is a favorite blade of many Klingons due to its being designed for use with a single hand, its lesser weight allowing its wielder to employ another sword or perhaps a *ghIntaq*, or even a shield, during personal combat. The *mek'leth*'s size can be a great advantage in situations where speed and maneuverability are of the essence. It also lends itself to easier concealment, a quality preferred by many experienced warriors.

Despite its versatility and popularity, the *mek'leth* is considered a weapon of choice for younger warriors, whereas their elders tend to rely on the larger, heavier *bat'leth* and the traditions surrounding the older weapon.

Mevak

Like the *d'k tahg*, the *mevak* is also a formidable blade despite its smaller size, though instead of being carried by individual warriors, its use instead is rooted in one of our oldest ceremonial rites, the *Mauk-to'Vor*. It is this ancient ceremony that permits a disgraced warrior to regain lost honor upon death and allows for his admittance to *Sto-Vo-Kor*, where he can continue waging war for all eternity against exalted foes. By ancient law, *Mauk-to'Vor* can be

performed only upon the request of the dishonored warrior, and it falls to his brother to carry out the ritual execution.

The *mevak* can also be used in the performance of the *hegh'bat* ceremony. When a Klingon has become injured or incapacitated to the point that he no longer can face his enemies as a warrior or when he has determined that he is nothing but a burden to his family, he may perform this ritual to take his own life. When the warrior is prepared to carry out the rite, the *mevak* is presented to him by his eldest son or a devoted friend. Once the dying Klingon plunges the knife into his own heart, the assistant then removes the blade and wipes it free of blood on his own sleeve, aiding the deceased warrior on his journey to *Sto-Vo-Kor*.

QhonDoq

Like the *qutluch*, this is a tool favored especially by some Klingons charged with carrying out assassinations. Many warriors scorn the *qhonDoq*, even refusing to call it a weapon, citing its size and the thinness of its blade. These qualities, they say, suggest that *qhonDoqs* are of interest only to cowards and others who prefer to attack from the shadows, rather than facing their enemies in open battle, courageously and with honor.

For a time, it was even believed that death by such a blade robbed a warrior of his honor and forbade him entrance to *Sto-Vo-Kor*, consigning him instead to the Barge of the Dead and ultimately to the depths of *Gre'thor* to suffer for all eternity at the hands of the beast Fek'lhr. To this day, noble Klingons welcome death by almost any other weapon over the *qhonDoq*.

Tajtiq

The *tajtiq* is another weapon with ties to ancient tradition. Longer than a knife, the short sword was ideal for ritual combat in which matters of honor were to be decided, often by the eldest siblings of rival houses. For such rituals, pairs of *tajtiqs* are typically commissioned based on requirements of the specific ceremony, with the weapons bearing the crests of the participating families.

Though viewed by many Klingons as an inadequate alternative to the *bat'leth* or the *mek'leth*, the *tajtiq* is taken into combat by many warriors as supplements to their weapons of choice. Like those more popular blades, the *tajtiq* is a common target for collectors within and beyond the Empire.

Tik'leth

Possessing a long, wide blade similar to that of the *d'k tahg*, the *tik'leth* is preferred by those Klingons whose hands are so large as to make wielding a smaller knife impractical. Shorter and lighter than a *bat'leth* or even a *mek'leth*, the *tik'leth* is an elegant weapon, requiring a dexterity and grace usually at odds with the strength needed to proficiently employ those larger blades. It is commonly worn into battle in a scabbard across its owner's back, its single grip making it ideal for use singly or in pairs.

As with the *ghIntaq*, the Imperial Guards of ancient times once were renowned for their prowess with the *tik'leth*, devoting years to mastering the intricacies of such a refined blade. In spirited competition, guardsmen were frequent recipients of the coveted Victor Ranking trophy, which today is rivaled for prestige only by the Champion Standing award bestowed upon the winner of the *bat'leth* Competition held each year on Forcas III.

APPENDIX B
THE SIEGE OF JAT'YLN PASS:
A CASE STUDY

Seldom are wars fought with an eye toward history. This, at least, is the case for those charged with waging the actual battles, be they in space or on the ground. Leaders of military actions are focused on victory, rather than providing fodder for reflection or classroom study. Nevertheless, confrontations provide not only lessons for future generations in how to better our understanding of warfare and how to fight, but also insight into those who took part in the original campaigns. Those who lead armies into battle might not understand at the time how their actions reflect the principles and precepts of war to which we Klingons subscribe. However, as students of history we are afforded the opportunity to scrutinize and assess these leaders' decisions as well as the resulting victories or defeats. In doing so, we are able to ascertain for ourselves how those warriors' choices influenced their battles, and how they typify—or fail to uphold—the teachings handed from Kahless through the centuries to us.

One battle worthy of such examination unfolded generations ago, well before we Klingons acquired the ability to travel beyond the confines of Qo'noS. This was an era when war was still largely fought face to face with one's enemy, and not so far removed from a time when the only weapons upon which a warrior could rely were those forged by his own hands or those of a trusted brother. So successful was this battle's execution of what now are regarded as time-honored military tactics—along with improvisational stratagems and pivotal judgment—that the events of what has come to be known as the Siege of Jat'yln Pass remain required learning for students of the Elite Command Academy.

It was during our Second Dynasty that General Kovatch, leader of House Zin'zeQ, attempted to overthrow the reign of Emperor Reclaw and claim the throne for himself. Upon learning of this plot and Kovatch's gathering of loyal forces in preparation for his campaign, Reclaw made the decision to launch a preemptive assault on the disloyal general's forces before they could be organized. Though the Emperor's advisors recommended attacks against vulnerable targets on the outskirts of territory claimed by Kovatch, this counsel was challenged by the suggestions of a younger officer, Commander Kam'pok, who instead advised a bold strike into the heart of the Emperor's newfound enemy and against Kovatch himself.

The generals scoffed at this notion, but Kam'pok pressed his appeal. A student of military history and of the Empire's conquests from his earliest days as an officer, Kam'pok was known and regarded for his unusual, even novel, views on warfare. So convinced was the commander of the merits of his plan that he volunteered to lead the assault, citing the extensive, unforgiving training to which he had subjected himself and the soldiers under his command in preparation for such a battle. While he and his staff finalized their preparations, Reclaw and his generals continued refining their own battle plan, readying it for action should Kam'pok fail. On the face of it, Kam'pok's approach to the coming battle can easily be accorded with the Fourth Precept: **Seek adversity.** In point of fact, and only through the luxury of retrospection, do we know that the commander's daring strategy would come to embody the wisdom of the First Precept: **Choose your enemies well.**

In an age before transporters, sensors, orbital bombardment or even transport vessels capable of ferrying hundreds of soldiers, Klingons marched to war over land, emerged from the sea, or descended from the air, *bat'leth* or crossbow at the ready. So it was that Commander Kam'pok, under cover of darkness, led a contingent of fewer than six hundred warriors against Kovatch and what later was determined to be several thousand soldiers, these but a fraction of the forces the general was assembling for his planned offensive against the First City. Given the Emperor's reluctance to fully embrace Kam'pok's plan, only the barest of resources were allocated to deliver the commander and his troops to the point of the intended assault. In short order, Kam'pok found himself having to split his own forces into smaller groups, each to be ferried in rapid succession to the targeted area using the limited number of aircraft at his disposal.

Hampering Kam'pok's efforts was the focal point of his assault proposal. Given the code designation "Jat'yln Pass," his target was little more than a small clearing amid dense jungle where Kovatch and his main forces were believed to be massing. Though it was the only open area for several kellicams in any direction, its size ensured that only a three transport aircraft could be accommodated at any one time. While lesser leaders might have balked at this apparent hindrance, perhaps electing to wait until more favorable conditions presented themselves, Kam'pok rejected such thinking, having already committed himself to the campaign. This decision personifies what we now revere as the Seventh Precept: **Leave nothing until tomorrow.**

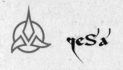

On the day of the attack and following a concentrated artillery bombardment of the surrounding jungle, the initial trio of transport craft landed at Jat'yln Pass. Kam'pok was the first to enter the combat area, armed as was his penchant with his pistol, the *d'k tahg* given to him by his father, and the *bat'leth* which had been carried by the warriors of his family for more than a dozen generations. Their arrival was not unanticipated or unnoticed, and within moments of landing, Kam'pok and his initial group of fifty warriors found themselves under fire from the surrounding jungle. Still, the level of resistance was light enough for Kam'pok to conclude that they were being engaged only by a small force. Not content simply to hold their positions while waiting for the reinforcements coming to him from the next wave of transports, Kam'pok knew that his enemy also would be augmenting their own numbers in short order.

Having foreseen this contingency, he deployed his soldiers across the clearing, establishing a defensive perimeter while sending reconnaissance parties into the jungle to seek out and close with their enemies. It was this action that allowed for the suppression of the small number of opposing combatants firing on them. This included the capture of several enemy soldiers, who in turn provided valuable intelligence about the location of Kovatch and his larger attack force, as well as the information that more enemy troops were on the way. With a choice to wait for more reinforcements while securing his own position, Kam'pok instead opted to send his warriors deeper into the jungle, continuing to push the defensive perimeter outward from the Jat'yln Pass. In this, the commander and his soldiers embraced the Third Precept: **Always face your enemy.**

With the initial opposition thwarted and the short-term advantage now belonging to him, Kam'pok continued to expand his growing perimeter as more of his own soldiers were delivered into the Pass. At the same time, early reports from his reconnaissance scouts told him that more of Kovatch's soldiers were moving into position in an attempt to envelop and divide the infiltrating force, while overwhelming the Pass itself in the hopes of denying further reinforcements access to the landing area. Kam'pok had trained his warriors well, empowering his subordinate officers and soldiers with the authority to analyze and adapt their own tactics to evolving situations without waiting for him to provide instructions or approval. Though his tactics are well-known and highly regarded by today's accepted principles of combat, at the time Kam'pok's unconventional methods succeeded in catching Kovatch almost wholly unprepared. Vulnerabilities quickly were exposed, which Kam'pok's warriors exploited to devastating effect. Many of the general's soldiers fell during these numerous, swift and surprising engagements as Kam'pok's warriors adhered to the Sixth Precept: **Destroy weakness**, targeting their enemies' deficiencies.

As dictated by the acknowledged doctrine and leadership philosophies of the time, the officers under General Kovatch's command were operating under a more standard, unified hierarchy, in which orders were communicated from the highest levels down through the ranks. It was a time-tested approach that had proven effective for overseeing most typical ground campaigns of the era, as large contingents faced off against one another on a designated field of battle.

On this day, such traditional thinking proved a major impediment for Kovatch, who soon found himself unable to respond in timely fashion to the rapid maneuvering of Kam'pok's smaller forces, which were moving independently of one another and pursuing their own mission objectives rather than focusing on a single identifiable goal. In many instances, this resulted in short, intense skirmishes that yielded numerous casualties among Kovatch's troops, while Kam'pok's soldiers avoided significant losses. The constant, intensive training to which the commander had subjected his soldiers was vindicated by his warriors' ability to proceed from engagement to engagement without tiring, all while giving Kovatch's soldiers no quarter. To an individual, the Klingons under Kam'pok's command exuded the spirit of the Second Precept: **Strike quickly or strike not.**

Kam'pok's nonconformist scheme was quick to garner rewards. After defeating the initial resistance and obtaining valuable information with which to augment his strategy, his subordinate officers began claiming their own victories. First was the attacking and securing of an artillery weapons emplacement, which quickly was put to use harassing Kovatch's forces and circumventing their attempts to trap the Jat'yln Pass in a flanking maneuver. The opportune acquisition of the artillery would prove to be a turning point in the battle.

Kam'pok, himself a warrior who had advanced through the ranks of the infantry to his current post, was not content to oversee or coordinate the developing battle from a central location. Instead, he led his own charges against Kovatch's forces. According to one of the many stories, songs, and legends inspired by the Siege of Jat'yln Pass, "Kam'pok fought as though possessed by the very spirit of Kahless. He spat into the face of the enemy and dared it to vanquish him, and that enemy could only tremble in fear." His courage not only stirred the warriors who followed him into battle but also demonstrated his personification of the Fifth Precept: **Reveal your true self in combat.**

qeS'a'

It was this bravery that ultimately brought Kam'pok face to face with Kovatch himself. In the middle of the steaming jungle, the two warriors brought their *bat'leths* to bear against one another in mortal combat only one could survive. Though Kovatch delivered a deadly strike, the point of his *bat'leth* sinking deep into his rival's chest, Kam'pok remained on his feet and was able to inflict his own killing blow, severing the general's head and denying him the opportunity to witness his opponent's passing. Only then did he allow death to claim him. With the final beats of his warrior's heart, as the last breath left his lungs, Kam'pok showed those who followed or opposed him the true meaning of the Ninth Precept: **Die standing up.**

In the wake of their leaders' deaths, both sides of the battle at Jat'yln Pass reacted in remarkably different ways. With Kovatch's soldiers still reacting to the increasing number of enemy soldiers in their midst, the warriors trained by Kam'pok continued to take the fight to their adversaries. As they pressed their attacks, their tenacity more than compensating for their inferior numbers, Kam'pok's executive officer, Lieutenant Mortas, took command of the seized artillery weapon and used it to keep Kovatch's soldiers at bay. This in turn acted as a signal to reinforcements, who were able to direct aerial bombardment on the targeted area, all but crushing the opposing force and sending it retreating into the jungle.

Now convinced that Kam'pok's plan had worked as the commander had envisioned, Emperor Reclaw directed even greater forces to continue what Kam'pok and his warriors had begun. In the wake of Kovatch's death, the planned overthrow of the Emperor fell apart. Those soldiers who had pledged to him their loyalty and who survived the Siege of Jat'yln Pass were stripped of their rank and honor, banished forever from service to the Empire. By imperial decree, the surviving members of House Zin'zeQ were imprisoned and the house itself dissolved, allowed never again to tarnish the honor of the Great Houses.

In the aftermath of the failed rebellion, Emperor Reclaw posthumously awarded Kam'pok the Star of Kahless and elevated his rank from Commander to Brigadier. A statue of the honored warrior now stands in the Hall of Heroes. His courage and devotion not only to the Empire but also to the warriors he commanded is a standard every leader strives to meet, and the tactics Kam'pok devised continue to influence military strategy—and strategic thinking—to this day.

APPENDIX C
THE SEARCH FOR THE
HISTORICAL KAHLESS

BY ANNABELLA FALCI

Professor Falci gave this talk on the search for the historical Kahless at McKay University on Mars, during a Day of Honor celebration at the university in 2383. Falci is a tenured professor in the Cultural Anthropology department at McKay, with a focus on Klingon studies. She's one of the Federation's leading experts on Klingon culture and lived within the Klingon Empire for a time. Born on Cestus III in 2318, she earned her bachelor's and master's degrees in Cultural Anthropology at Doragon University on Berengaria and her doctorate in the same at Fordham University on Earth. She moved to Qo'noS in 2364, and lived on various worlds in the Empire until 2372, when Chancellor Gowron expelled all Federation citizens and diplomats and the Empire temporarily withdrew from the Khitomer Accords. Returning to the Federation, she joined the teaching staff at McKay, receiving tenure in 2379. She has occasionally served as a consultant to the Federation Diplomatic Corps and to the administrations of Presidents Zife and Bacco.

Throughout the Galaxy, we have found that many species have some manner of spiritual beliefs that involve paying homage to unseen, powerful beings imbued with a level of divinity. The basic pattern is remarkably similar on many worlds. Sentient beings all have a tendency to ascribe supernatural origins to phenomena they cannot explain.

In some cases, those origins lie with beings who are further (or at least differently) evolved and who are considered powerful god-like creatures. For example, the Greek pantheon on Earth was revealed in the 23rd century to be made up of alien beings with unusual control over matter and energy. They came to Earth and became the basis of one group of people's mythology. There are the Prophets of Bajoran myth and legend, who were revealed to be the aliens living inside the Bajoran wormhole. There is the Demiurge of the Aenar on Andor, which was discovered recently to be an actual being of energy who created the genetic code for the Aenar millennia ago. And then of course there are the Founders of the Dominion, who claimed divinity and genetically bred the Vorta and the Jem'Hadar to spread their word, as it were.

Some religious beliefs are centered on historical figures who are either divine or who are said to have a connection to the divine: for example, Jesus Christ on Earth, the Emissary on Bajor, and the Speaker of Death on Nasat. Most of those personages—including the three I just named—can be considered messengers for a divine being. Jesus is the son of the Christian monotheistic God and a human woman, the Emissary is the messenger of the Prophets, the Speaker of Death is a conduit for messages from the afterlife, and so on. One can even argue that Surak of Vulcan holds a similar place as that culture's mytho-historical figure; Surak's role in Vulcan history is revered due to his bringing the concepts of logic and order to the fore in a chaotic world. Even there, though, Surak is not the divine figure—indeed, most Vulcans would scoff at the very notion, viewing divine beings as part of the pre-Surak barbarism that nearly destroyed their world. But one could argue that Vulcans revere logic with the same intensity (I almost said *fervor,* but that word would be inappropriate) with which many other species revere their divine beings.

Then we have the Klingons, who have, in Kahless, a messianic figure very much like those listed in the previous paragraph. Like Surak, Kahless united his homeworld under a philosophical code. Like Jesus, he died with the promise of resurrection, and his believers await his return (though clerics did manufacture an attempt at his return, about which more in a moment). And like the Speaker of Death, he provides guidance in how his people face death.

I'm cherry-picking, of course—the overlap among all these figures is significant—but what's special about Kahless is that he has been imbued with divinity by the Klingons, a divinity that does not derive from another divine source the way that all those listed above, save Surak, claim to. But Surak himself is not considered divine, and what's more, his life and times are fairly well chronicled. While it is not complete—as an example, the discovery of the coronet of Karatek revealed new information about Surak's life—it is enough to be able to paint a decent picture of what Surak was like.

Of Kahless, however, there is less certainty. Until comparatively recently, Klingon history was recorded primarily through oral tradition, a notoriously unreliable method for preserving facts. Add to that the reverence that Klingons hold for the personage of Kahless and it makes it difficult to filter historical fact from hagiographical storytelling.

We do know that someone who is now called Kahless did exist at the time when Kahless the Unforgettable is alleged to have lived. For that, we have

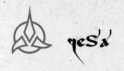

the Knife of Kirom to thank. That blade was stained with the blood of Kahless, and a clone of Kahless that looked exactly like the contemporary portraits of Kahless was a genetic match for the blood on the knife. The clerics who created the clone did not have access to the Knife of Kirom, which means they used other genetic material to create the clone. (The exact material was lost when the cloning facility on Boreth was destroyed during Morjod's attempted coup against Chancellor Martok in 2375, right after the Dominion War ended.) This means there are (or were) at least two biological samples of the original Kahless—or of a person who looks like Kahless's depictions.

The written stories we have of Kahless are all of dubious historical credibility, unfortunately. Klingons value the importance of a good story over historicity, and so embellishment is generally considered an important component of the tale. As an example, I once had the honor of meeting *Dahar* Master Kor when he was Klingon Ambassador to Vulcan during a reception at an academic conference. He told a story of his discovery of the Delta Triangle. As it happens, I've read the records of that incident, which also involved a Starfleet vessel. While the broad strokes of Kor's description were more or less the same as the details in the log entries, the two sources differed considerably. And all those differences were in service of making Kor's role more important, his accomplishments more impressive, and of downplaying any positive accomplishments by those who opposed him (both the Starfleet captain, James Kirk, and the Elysian Council that ruled the territory within the triangle).

Given the reverence Klingons hold for Kahless, it becomes that much harder to sift out the historical truth from the stories about him that have been told, and recorded in the sacred texts, in the *Book of Honor* (or *paq'batlh*), and in *The Klingon Art of War* (or *qeS'a'*).

For example, the story of how Kahless forged the first *bat'leth* was first revealed to the general public when the clone of Kahless was unveiled. Only the clerics knew that story, meant to test Kahless when he returned, though, of course, the clone only knew it because those selfsame clerics programmed it into his memory so that he could tell the story to "prove" that he was truly Kahless. But the story is patently absurd: supposedly Kahless shoved a lock of his hair into a river of lava from a volcano and then molded it into the very first *bat'leth*, known today as the Sword of Kahless.

A few years later, during the aforementioned coup by Morjod, the Sword of Kahless was recovered by Chancellor Martok, who still wields it today.

However, that *bat'leth*, which dates back to the time of Kahless, was very obviously forged by a smith. The imperfections show that it was forged by hand rather than by machine, but there are definite indications of formal forging—and also no biological traces inside the blade to indicate its origin as a lock of hair. Furthermore, the Sword of Kahless showed no indication of being heavily used prior to Martok's recovery of it. Only the faintest traces of blood were on it, which is odd for a weapon that Kahless supposedly used so many times in battle, particularly against Molor's forces at Qam-Chee.

Speaking of Molor, another of the most popular stories of Kahless was, if not disproven, at the very least called into question after the destruction of Praxis. One location that suffered severe damage from the moon's explosion was Qa'varin, the fortress from which the tyrant Molor ruled until he was defeated by Kahless.

Molor was one of many warlords who ruled a region of Qo'noS in the time before Kahless, and he had by far the most territory. Though he is often spoken of with disdain due to his opposition of Kahless, in truth there is little evidence to support the notion that he was any worse—or any better—than any of the other warlords, only that he was more successful. Several whose cruelty to their subjects was far greater, or whose corruption at the expense of their subjects was far more lavish, are not spoken of with the same disgust, because they capitulated to Kahless or lost to him in what was deemed honorable combat.

Kahless's defeat of Molor was the final victory that united Qo'noS, but the story of their final battle also is one that strains credulity. Kahless supposedly came upon Molor at his citadel at Qa'varin and they fought for many days until Kahless was victorious, beheading Molor with his *bat'leth*. Yet Kahless's mate, Lukara, and all his forces, not to mention Molor's own forces, just stood around and waited for them to finish fighting?

In the aftermath of Praxis's explosion, Qa'varin, which had been converted to a shrine to Kahless, was badly damaged. The lower regions had been sealed off centuries ago, and exposing them released a pathogen into the air, identified as *Dir rop*, or "skin disease," something that occasionally afflicts animals and Klingons alike. There was a record of such a plague among *minn'hor* beasts in Kahless's time. Once the region was decontaminated, a Federation medical team examined the ruins of the castle more closely. They found that the virus had lain dormant in the sealed region of Qa'varin and then became airborne after the seal was broken. They also found absolutely no evidence of any blood being spilled anywhere inside at any time, with the sole exception of some minute blood traces upon Molor's throne.

Also discovered in the sealed region was a decapitated body. Famously, Kahless *did* decapitate Molor, but it was supposed to be after a prolonged fight all across the battlements. While it is impossible to determine whether the decapitated body was Molor's, the body did come from that time period and was headless, and there is no record of what happened to Molor's body. Said corpse was also ravaged by *Dir rop*.

So it is possible that Kahless and Molor had no great battle. Kahless's victories against Molor might have been achieved, not through his innate superiority, but because Molor was dying of an illness. In the end, he may well have beheaded Molor, not as the culmination of days of honorable combat, but because his enemy was unable to put up much resistance.

Of course, I speak only in possibilities. If you tried to tell a Klingon this, they would say that the story is of far more import than the facts. Indeed, that was what the Klingons *did* say a century ago when these discoveries were made. And they would have an excellent point. I remember the first time I read the story of Kahless and Molor's final battle as it was chronicled in *qeS'a'*. I was utterly captivated by it. I loved the exchange between the two combatants, with Molor's refusal to surrender, despite the odds against him, because he refused to live in a world ruled by Kahless, and Kahless telling the most dishonorable figure in the sacred texts that he still had the opportunity to die with honor.

And all that is true, and we should not strive to take the Klingons' stories away from them. But still, one wonders who this person is who has become such an integral part of Klingon life that a group of clerics saw resurrecting him as a route to power.

On Earth, scholars attempting to learn about the historical figure of Jesus Christ (or Joshua ben Joseph, as he was more likely known to the people of the time) tend to start with texts with no allegiance to Christianity as it developed, specifically those of citizens of the Roman Empire. In a similar vein, my own studies have revealed that the most objective reports of Kahless can be found in the farthest reaches of Qo'noS, the lands that were among the last to pledge themselves to Kahless's banner.

For example, there are several references to Kahless in letters written by Kaprav and Vis'Ar, the citizens of the peninsula of Kalranz from whom Kahless learned *klin zha*. Only one letter talks about him in any depth, however, and it is from Vis'Ar to her mother and father. (In the following excerpt, "K." refers to Kahless and "The Game" refers to *klin zha*.)

"We met today again with K., who spoke again of his admiration for The Game. He was an apt student, learning The Game faster than anyone Kaprav and I have ever seen. He had booked passage on a wind boat home, but cancelled it so he could spend more time with us playing The Game. I must confess that K. has found more in The Game than we ever have, and his enthusiasm has, in turn, brought more joy to us in playing it. K. also joined us in watching a *tik'leth* demonstration. At one point, the instructor asked for volunteers from the crowd. We encouraged K. to respond to the call. He refused at first, saying he was only an observer, but when we finally talked him into it, he proved a poor hand with the sword. The instructor's techniques proved too complex for him, and he demurred, letting another volunteer take his place. After that, we dined at an eatery on the water and spoke all through the night of combat and honor and The Game. It was a great day with a man whose presence has deeply honored our lives."

Quite a far cry from the person held to be the greatest warrior in Klingon history. (Recall that it was the clone's defeat in combat with Chancellor Gowron that led to its exposure as a clone and not the true second coming of Kahless.) But this letter—which I only happened to find on a trip to the archives on Kalranz—as well as the lack of battle damage to the first *bat'leth*, indicates that the clone may have been a more accurate rendering of Kahless than was believed possible.

Kahless and his brother Morath supposedly fought for twelve days and twelve nights because Morath had dishonored his name by lying, or so we're told. Indeed, it's one of the great cautionary tales among Klingons, the story parents always tell their children when they want to remind them that to lie is to bring about dishonor.

Yet the story itself is almost certainly a lie. The Bazho River where the battle supposedly took place is now a calm body of water, due to the artificial creation of a branch in order to service a town suffering a drought about two centuries ago. As a result, most modern Klingons think of the Bazho River as a good place for a battle between two brothers, but in fact a prolonged battle at the location given in the story would have been impossible. The tides of the river were brutal, and there are many records of people (often trying to go to

the location where Kahless and Morath fought before the river was split) carried away if they stood too close. It is possible that the battle between the two took them close by, but it could not have been close to the river for longer than a few seconds, or else both participants would have been carried away by the river. Certainly, no one could have fought there for twelve days and nights. If the location of the battle is suspect, so too is the rest of the story.

On top of that, there are occasional mentions of Morath in documents that post-date the battle, including a report made by one of Kahless's generals about the final battle against Molor being led not by Kahless and Lukara, but by Kahless and Morath. There are other references as well, including one from Kalavat, a minor soldier in Kahless's army who eventually became a general. Kalavat said the last time he saw Kahless was right before his ascension to *Sto-Vo-Kor*, when he said goodbye to his brother, who should have been dead for several years.

Every quote attributed to Kahless, whether or not he actually said the words, revolves around honor and glory and duty and combat. Of those, skill in the last is the only thing that comes close to being measurable. We know that Kahless's teachings on the subject of the first three were very effective, so it is assumed that he was as skilled in the fourth. But who's to say he was? After all, what made Kahless great *wasn't* his ability to physically defeat his enemies. Molor did that, and he was reviled. Indeed, many of the most despised figures in Klingon history are warriors who were strong fighters with many victories to their names: Chang, Qorvak, Gamnaq, and so many others. No, what made Kahless stand out from other Klingons was that his words carried meaning, that they still do.

And ultimately, that's what matters. No matter who he might have really been.

ACKNOWLEDGMENTS

First off, thanks to Dayton Ward, who put me together with Ben Grossblatt of becker&mayer! in the first place, and who also added his own magnificent contribution to this volume.

Secondly, thanks to Ben himself. This was my first time working with the good Mr. Grossblatt, and he is a fine and noble editor with whom it was a joy to work. I must also thank Ed Schlesinger at Simon & Schuster and John Van Citters at CBS—it was far from my first time working with either of them, and their feedback was, as always, truly excellent. And of course, my wonderful agent, Lucienne Diver, who keeps the paperwork flowing freely.

Many writers have contributed to making the Klingons the nifty creatures they are today, primary among them Gene L. Coon, who created them for "Errand of Mercy" on the original series, John M. Ford, who developed the culture in the seminal novel *The Final Reflection*, and Ronald D. Moore, who did so much work with the species on three spinoffs. I also have done quite a bit with the Klingons over the years. But credit must also go to the following writers and artists who did honor to the Klingons onscreen and in prose and comics form, and whose work was a huge influence on this volume: Ira Steven Behr, Jerome Bixby, Brannon Braga, Rene Echevarria, Denny Martin Flinn, Michael Jan Friedman (especially his novel *Kahless*), David Gerrold, David A. Goodman, David Messina, Nicholas Meyer, Peter Pachoumis, Melinda M. Snodgrass (who gave us K'Ratak in the *Star Trek: The Next Generation* episode "The Measure of a Man"), Scott & David Tipton, Robert Hewitt Wolfe, and JK Woodward. I must also give thanks and praise to Dan Curry, the visual effects supervisor on *The Next Generation* (among others) who created the *bat'leth* and developed *mok'bara*. And the actors who've played Klingons over the years, in particular Michael Ansara (Kang), James Avery (K'Vagh), William Campbell (Koloth), John Colicos (Kor), Charles Cooper (Koord and K'mpec), Roxann Dawson (B'Elanna Torres), Michael Dorn (Worf), David Graf (Leskit), J. G. Hertzler (Martok and Kolos), Susan Howard (Mara), Barbara March (Lursa), Patrick Massett (Duras), Robert O'Reilly (Gowron), Suzie Plakson (K'Ehleyr), Christopher Plummer (Chang), Ned Romero (Krell), John Schuck (the Klingon Ambassador), Brian Thompson (Klag), Tony Todd (Kurn), John Vickery (Orak), and Gwynyth Walsh (B'Etor).

I also owe a massive debt to two dear friends, Marc Okrand, the creator of the Klingon language for *Star Trek III: The Search for Spock*, and Dr. Lawrence Schoen, the head of the Klingon Language Institute, an organization that has done much to build on Marc's work. Various reference works were also of great use, notably the Memory Alpha and Memory Beta wikis online and *Star Charts* by Geoffrey Mandel.

Thanks also to GraceAnne Andreassi DeCandido (a.k.a. The Mom), Wrenn Simms, Tina Randleman, David Mack, and Dale Mazur, for various and sundry bits of assistance. And thanks to all the animals in my life, who have helped me out by laying around and looking cute: Scooter, Belle, Sterling, Rhiannon, and the late, lamented Newcastle.

ABOUT THE AUTHOR

Keith R. A. DeCandido has written dozens of works of *Star Trek* fiction focusing on the Klingons, including the novels *Diplomatic Implausibility*, *A Good Day to Die*, *Honor Bound*, *Enemy Territory*, *A Burning House*, and *The Art of the Impossible*; the short stories "*loDnI'pu' vavpu' je*" in *Tales from the Captain's Table*, "Family Matters" in *Mirror Universe: Shards and Shadows*, and "The Unhappy Ones" in *Seven Deadly Sins*; and the comic book *Alien Spotlight: Klingons*. That's just a part of his ledger of *Trek* fiction, which also includes stories based on each of the five TV series, a couple of political novels, some alternate universe tales, and much more, including the *USA Today* best-selling *The Next Generation* novel *A Time for War, a Time for Peace*, which told the story of the events leading up to the final *TNG* movie *Nemesis*. Currently, he's doing a Rewatch of *Deep Space Nine* on Tor. com, having completed a similar Rewatch of *TNG* from 2011-2013 on the site. Keith has also written in more than a dozen other media universes, ranging from TV shows (*Buffy the Vampire Slayer*, *Doctor Who*, *Leverage*, *Supernatural*, and more) to games (*Command and Conquer*, *Dungeons & Dragons*, *StarCraft*, *World of Warcraft*) to movies (*Cars*, *Kung Fu Panda*, *Resident Evil*, *Serenity*) and to comic books (the Hulk, the Silver Surfer, Spider-Man, the X-Men). In 2009, he was granted a Lifetime Achievement Award by the International Association of Media Tie-in Writers, which means he never needs to achieve anything ever again.

In addition, Keith has several of his own universes floating around, including a series of fantasy police procedurals: the acclaimed novels *Dragon Precinct*, *Unicorn Precinct*, *Goblin Precinct*, *Gryphon Precinct*, *Mermaid Precinct*, and the short story collection *Tales from Dragon Precinct*. Other recent and upcoming work ranges from *Leverage: The Zoo Job* to "The Ballad of Big Charlie" in Jonathan Maberry's *V-Wars* to the SCPD series of cop novels set in a city filled with super-heroes to *Ragnarok and Roll: Tales of Cassie Zukav*, to *Weirdness Magnet*, a collection of urban fantasy stories set in Key West.

When he isn't writing fiction, Keith is a podcaster (*The Chronic Rift*, *HG World*, *Gypsy Cove*, *Dead Kitchen Radio: The Keith R. A. DeCandido Podcast*), a second-degree black belt in karate, and probably some other stuff that he can't remember due to lack of sleep. He lives in New York City with two humans, one dog, three cats, and way too many books. Find out less at his cheerfully retro web site DeCandido.net, which is a portal to pretty much everything he does.